SO-ADJ-020

# THE BOY CAPTIVE OF OLD DEERFIELD

## MARY P. WELLS SMITH

www.gideonhousebooks.com

# THE BOY CAPTIVE OF OLD DEERFIELD

Mary P. Wells Smith

**© 2016 Gideon House Books**

All rights reserved. No part of this publication may be reproduced, stored in a retrieval system or transmitted in any form or by any means, electronic, mechanical, photocopying, recording or otherwise without the prior permission of the publisher or in accordance with the provisions of the Copyright, Designs and Patents Act 1988 or under the terms of any licence permitting limited copying issued by the Copyright Licensing Angency.

**Published by:**
Gideon House Books
5518 Flint St. Shawnee KS 66203
www.gideonhousebooks.com

**Typesetting & Cover Design:** Josh Pritchard

**ISBN-13:** 978-1-943133-71-0

# CONTENTS

1. In October, 1703. . . . . . . . . . . . . . . 5

2. Captured. . . . . . . . . . . . . . . 15

2. Wedding . . . . . . . . . . . . . . . 23

4. A New Arrival . . . . . . . . . . . . . 31

5. A Warning Omen . . . . . . . . . . . 41

6. The Blow Falls . . . . . . . . . . . . . 49

7. The Captives . . . . . . . . . . . . . 59

8. On to the North . . . . . . . . . . . . 67

9. Dividing the Captives . . . . . . . . . . 75

10. An Unexpected Pleasure . . . . . . . . 83

11. Sunday in the Wilderness . . . . . . . 91

12. A False Alarm . . . . . . . . . . . . . 97

13. Alone with the Indians . . . . . . . . . 105

14. Farther On . . . . . . . . . . . . . . 113

15. Meeting Old Friends . . . . . . . . . 119

16. After a Fast, a Feast . . . . . . . . . . 127

17. A Tedious Day's Travel . . . . . . . . . 135

18. The Boys Hunt . . . . . . . . . . . . 141

19. Lost in the Woods . . . . . . . . . . . 151

20. Nunganey's Trick . . . . . . . . . . . 159

21. The Bear Hunt . . . . . . . . . . . . 167

22. Changed Plans . . . . . . . . . . . . 175

# 1

# IN OCTOBER, 1703

OCTOBER in Deerfield was never more beautiful than in this autumn of 1703. The little settlement of forty houses brooded under what seemed the protecting shadow of Pocumtuck Mountain; the river winding through the smiling meadows; the "Sunsick Mountains" beyond rising in brilliant splendor against the deep blue of the western sky: all combined in one picture of peaceful beauty.

The crops having been garnered, on October 1st the meadows had been thrown open to the stock of the settlers. During the summer the cattle, each branded with its owner's initials, had run in the woods on Pocumtuck Mountain in wild freedom, save as the milk cows were sent out daily in the care of a cow-herd who guarded them by day and brought them home at night. But now the cattle revelled in the ease, safety, and rich pasturage of the home meadows. No more searching for scanty patches of rank wild grass through the mazes of the forest, torn by bush and brier, crowding among huge trees and rocks that often hid wild bear, or panther ready to spring on the defenseless creatures. The evident content and satisfaction of the happy animals scattered over the green meadows, cropping the sweet grass, or lying basking in the autumn sunlight as they chewed their cud, added to the peacefulness of the scene.

But the peace was in nature, not in the hearts of the anxious settlers.

After supper, on the night of October 7th, Rev. John Williams, the Deerfield minister, said to his wife:

"'Tis a week today, Eunice, since the cattle were led into the meadows, and as yet I have not been out to look after mine. Benoni Stebbins says he thinks some of mine are missing. He saw but four with my brand. I am going out this evening to investigate the matter."

"Oh, father," cried Stephen, a boy of ten, "I wish could go with you!"

"Do not speak of such a thing," said the mother, whose still young and pleasing face showed lines of care and anxiety. "I would not even suffer Samuel, your big brother, to go. 'T is surely bad enough to have your father thus expose himself. If you feel that you must go, John, would far rather you went by daylight. Cannot you wait until tomorrow?"

"No, Eunice. 'T is not thought safe for any one of us to venture outside the palisades in the daytime. Here under our mountain, our town plot and meadows all lie exposed to the view of the enemy, who can lie hid in ambush on that height and fall upon us at their pleasure. T is considered much safer to go forth at night. Remember, good wife, that the Lord careth for us. The darkness and the light are both alike to Him."

"Yes, I know that," said the wife. "Yet, nevertheless, I shall suffer constant anxiety until I see you safely home again."

"I would I could have gone too," still persisted Stephen, standing in the doorway, watching his father, as, carrying his gun, the settlers' constant companion, he rode away into the thick shadows of the night. He was visible for a little while in the light glimmering from the windows of the houses within the stockade. Then he disappeared through the fort's northern gateway.

"I am so tired of being pent up here in the stockade," continued Stephen, as he slowly closed the door and came in. "So are the other boys. Today, Sam Stebbins and Jonathan Hoyt and John Catlin, and the other big boys, dared Ebenezer Sheldon and Joseph Kellogg and me to go out on the mountain nutting with them some day this week."

"Stephen!" exclaimed his mother. "I hope you were not tempted, even for a moment, by any such wild scheme. 'T would be as much as your lives are worth! I wonder at the foolhardiness of those boys!"

"John said they would go but a little way outside the palisades. And Sam and Jonathan poohed at all this talk about Indians; said none had even been seen around here for a long while. They said folks were silly, they thought, to be frightened because there had been some Indian troubles down in Maine. They thought the best way was to go ahead and not be so afraid. They weren't afraid."

"Great wiseacres they, forsooth," said the mother. "They had best listen to older and wiser folk, who have had sorry experience with the Indians long before they were born. Have a care, Stephen. Should you be tempted to disobey, you know your father will not spare the rod of correction."

"Yes, I know that full well," said Stephen, with a shrug of his shoulders, as at unpleasant reminiscences, while Samuel, a boy of fifteen, who had just come in, hearing part of the conversation, said:

"Remember the Beldings, Stephen."

"I'm tired of hearing about the Beldings," said Stephen. "We are always being reminded of their capture. 'T is as much as seven years since they were carried off, and there has been no trouble with the Indians to speak of since. I think just as Jonathan Hoyt does, that people are too scared."

"Young cockerels ever crow the loudest," said the mother. "Our youths must be guided by their elders, many of whom have had sad experience of the Indians' craftiness. They are so sly and subtle. All may seem fair smiling, yet suddenly, in the twinkling of an eye, enemy fall on us when we least dream of it. Since the post brought word that news had been received in Boston of war declared again between France and England, your father and all the leading men have suffered sore uneasiness here in this lonely outpost. I pray their fears may prove unnecessary. Yet I can but be most anxious."

"I guess the Governor of New York State and Major Schuyler of Albany know full as much about it as Jonathan and Sam," here spoke up Esther Williams, a girl of thirteen. "They sent word by post to Deerfield that Indians were coming down from Canada to attack us, and warned us to be on our guard."

"That was last May, full five months ago," said Stephen, "and naught has come of it yet."

"Thank God that naught has," said the mother, fervently. "I do not like, Stephen, to hear you speak so lightly of such grave matters."

"They that know nothing fear nothing," whispered Esther in Stephen's ear.

"Stephen had best not be too forward and bold, or he will be ordered out, first he knows, to work on repairing our fortifications," said Samuel. "Some folk feel so worried about their dilapidated condition that I expect soon even the little boys will be called out to help us. I tell you, mother," continued Samuel, as he drew a chair up to the table, "I'm tired and hungry; hungry enough to eat raw bear's meat, I verily believe. I've been tugging at heavy logs and planks all day."

"Esther," said Mrs. Williams, "bring your brother a porringer of that bean porridge I saved hot for him over the fire. And Eunice, you can help. Run out in the kitchen for a loaf of bread."

Eunice, a bright little girl of seven, pleased to think she was helping, willingly ran for the bread, and was rewarded by the hungry Sam with some fresh chestnuts he had picked up in the woods while working on the palisades.

Parthena, the negro slave woman, was busy in the kitchen, getting supper for her husband, Frank, who, like Samuel, had been out all day helping repair the palisades. The fortifications had become weak and decayed, and since war had again been declared, the settlers were trying to repair them.

"I was awful scared today." Frank told his wife, out in the back kitchen, where he was eating supper with the keen zest of a man who had worked out-doors all day in the sharp autumn air. "I had to go out chopping trees on the mountain, way outside the palisades."

"Mercy sakes, Frank! I don't wonder you were scared," said Parthena.

"That didn't scare me," said Frank. "We had a squad of soldiers to guard us, who kept watch every minute. But one time I went off in the woods by myself, beyond the guard, to cut down a big oak tree, the biggest one anywhere around."

"That was risky," said Parthena.

"All of a sudden, I happened to look up and I saw a bush a-shaking."

"The wind blew it, I reckon," said Parthena.

"No, everything was dead still. There wasn't a breath of air stirring. As soon as I saw that bush a-moving, says to myself, 'There's something wrong. That's either Indians or ghosts, and I don't want to meet either of 'em.' I quit my big oak in a hurry, and went back to work behind the guard."

"You didn't see any Indians?"

"No. But, I tell you, that bush wasn't shaking itself."

"All this talk about Indians is enough to scare folks out of their wits," said Parthena. "I declare, I'm most afraid to go out to the well for water after sundown."

John and Warham Williams, the minister's youngest children, little boys of six and four, sitting on the settle before the fire, had ceased playing, and lay back lazily in the warmth of the flickering firelight, looking suspiciously sleepy. Eunice, in her warm seat in the inglenook, was yawning over the New England Primer. Tomorrow her father intended to exercise the children in the catechism, and her mother had been helping the little girl in its study.

"'Tis quite time my little men were tucked into their trundle-bed," said the mother, lovingly.

"No, no, mother; I'm not a bit sleepy." said John, making a brave effort to look wide-awake.

But little Warham slipped along to his mother's side, and laid his sleepy head on her lap, too far gone to protest.

"Eunice, let me hear you say your verse now," said her mother, taking the Primer, while Eunice repeated, in droning, sleepy tone:

> "Good children must
> Fear God all Day,     Love Christ alway,
> Parents obey,     In Secret Pray,
> No false thing say,     Mind little Play,
> By no Sin stray,       Make no delay,
> In doing good."

Eunice said her verse without a mistake, closing with an irrepressible yawn.

"Very well, indeed, child," said her mother. "You will soon know your Primer. Poor children. You are all so sleepy. But I'm loath to put you to bed till your father returns, so that we may have the family prayers before you go. He should have been back ere this, I am sure. I pray no disaster has befallen him. Samuel, look out and see if he be in sight."

Samuel peered out the door into the night. Some of the houses within the stockade were already dark, for the tired settlers were glad to observe the first half of the old maxim "early to bed and early to rise," since stern necessity required them to practice the last half.

"I see naught stirring," Samuel reported, but the night-watch going past. Hark! he calls, 'Eight o' the clock, and all's well.'"

"I pray all be well with your poor father," said the anxious mother, but little comforted by the watchman's cheery cry.

Another hour passed. Mrs. Williams was obliged to send the younger children to bed. She sat before the fire, her fingers making her knitting-needles fly from force of habit, for the mother of a large and growing family in those times knew no idle moments.

Samuel, in spite of the fatigue of his long day's labor, and the drowsiness that made him nod at times as if he would fall into the fire, yet dutifully sat up to keep his mother company in her watch. Since his older brother, Eliezer, had gone away to Hadley to fit for Harvard College, he felt that upon him devolved the duties of the oldest son in so large a family, and his loving help was often a great comfort to his parents.

Parthena, also loyal to her beloved mistress, was trying to keep her tired eyes open by spinning at a wheel in the back of the room, though the wheel whirled rather fitfully, and not with the briskness she usually put into its revolutions.

By and by, Mrs. Williams, her ears strained to catch every sound, fancied she heard through the drowsy hum of the wheel the beat of horse's hoofs.

"Stop, Parthena," she cried, starting up. "Yes, 'tis plainly a horse's hoofs. Run, Samuel, and unbolt the door. I pray that be your father."

It was indeed Mr. Williams who had just ridden up. The wife, at her first glance, saw that he looked pale and troubled.

"I will put up your horse, father," said Samuel.

"'Tis best I go with you, my son," said the father, gun in hand. "We will be back in a moment, wife. Bolt the door at once. We will come in the back way."

Mrs. Williams well knew from her husband's face that something had happened. But as she did not wish Parthena frightened, she said to her:

"You can go to bed now, Parthena. 'T is very late, and I know you are tired and sleepy. Since I have my husband safely back again, I shall need your faithful attendance no longer."

"Good-night, Mistress Williams," said Parthena, departing with a gusty yawn that threatened to extinguish the candle in her hand.

"What is it, John? What has happened?" asked Mrs. Williams, as her husband and Samuel now entered, her husband limping, and leaning on Samuel's shoulder.

"I fear I ran a narrow chance of capture by Indians this night but for the Lord's watchful care," said Mr. Williams, as he gave Samuel his gun to replace on the hooks over the mantel-piece, where it always hung, ready for instant use.

"O husband, do you really mean it?" cried the wife.

"Yes, even so. I rode out past the houses north of the stockade and then turned off to the westward near Broughton's Hill. Benoni told me he saw some of my cattle today near Broughton's Pond. There was a bright afterglow tonight, and the daylight still lingered faintly in the west, so that, after I was away from the lights of the houses, I could discern moving objects, though indistinctly. I alighted as I neared the pond, leading my horse, thinking to examine the bushes more closely."

"John, that was most rash!" exclaimed the wife.

"As I approached a clump of bushes, suddenly my horse began to sniff and start, pulling on the bridle and showing signs of great uneasiness. I bethought me at once of Indians, though I saw not a sign of any. But at that moment, saw some dark objects crawling forth from under the clump of bushes."

"May it not have been some of the creatures,—sheep, perchance?" suggested the wife.

"Nay, those were no four-footed beasts, though they meant me to think them such. They were Indians lying in ambush, and crawling out on all fours till they could get near enough to seize me. Doubtless, they heard my horse's footfall from afar. I hastened to remount, in my hurry stumbling over a rolling log, and I fear spraining my ankle. But I managed to remount, and putting spurs to my horse, who, in truth, needed no urging, I galloped back to David Hoyt's house. There I stopped, as none pursued me, to warn Deacon Hoyt and the Beldings and Stebbinses and Kelloggs and all those living north of the stockade to be on the alert. Some of them say they will move into the stockade as soon as they can get shelter here. Their women especially are afraid to live longer so exposed."

"'T is little wonder," said the wife. "But, John, I still cannot help hoping that you were deceived; that those were not really Indians you saw."

"I would I could think so," said Mr. Williams. "But I am certain by the conduct of my horse, if naught else, that they were indeed Indians, and that I had a most providential escape. But now, wife, if you will give my aching ankle some attention, we will have our prayers and to bed. Whate'er betides, we must not omit to thank God for my merciful deliverance out of the enemies' hands, and crave His watchful care over us and our poor exposed settlement during the dangers of the darkness."

The next day the news that Mr. John Williams, their revered pastor, had narrowly escaped capture by Indians, spread like wildfire through the little settlement. Work was pushed on the feeble palisades with redoubled energy, Mr. Williams toiling with his people in what he felt to be such vitally important work.

That evening, Stephen, who had been sent by his father on an errand to Godfrey Nims, the neighbor dwelling in the opposite corner of the stockade, returned full of excitement.

"Father!" he exclaimed on entering the room, "what do you think? Zebediah Williams and his half-brother, John Nims, were just about going forth into the meadows when I came away! When the cow-herd brought the herd m tonight two of Mr. Nims's cows were missing, so Zebediah and John determined to go forth into the meadow and seek them."

"I pray they may escape harm and return in safety," said Mr. Williams, "but I am sorry they venture their lives so rashly after my experience of last night."

"In truth, John and Zebediah, two fearless young men, had taken but little stock in the minister's tale of Indians. When their father, Godfrey Nims, had doubted that it was safe for them to sally forth in search of the missing cows, John had said lightly:

"Father, you know well how overly anxious good Mr. Williams has been, ever since we knew war was again declared. The good man means well, but his feelings of anxious care and responsibility for his flock posted here so far out in the wilderness makes him unduly fearful in my opinion."

"Yes," said Zebediah, as he threw the strap of his powder-horn over his neck, and took down his gun, "and when you have Indians on the brain, 't is easy enough to see one behind every bush. I know that full well."

"I wish you would not go, Zebediah," pleaded his young wife, tears in her eyes.

"Don't be foolish, Sarah," said Zebediah, kissing the loving young face raised in pleading to his own. "'T is only good-by for an hour or two, and John and I will be back and to bed, with our cows safe under our own barn roof if we have good luck."

"Have no fears for us, mother," said John, cheerily, trying to reassure their anxious mother, as the two young men closed the door of home and walked away into the darkness.

# 2

# CAPTURED

TWO hours after the departure of the young men, the wife of Zebediah, going to the door for the second time, and peering anxiously out into the darkness, said:

"I wonder why Zebediah does not come home? I am certain something has happened to him."

"Give the boys time, daughter," said Godfrey Nims. "The cows may have wandered far."

"In truth, I too am beginning to feel worried about them." said Mrs. Nims.

"Pooh, pooh, mother," began Godfrey, when a running footstep was heard outside, and without the ceremony of knocking, the night watchman, pale and excited, burst into the room, crying:

"I heard the distant sound of guns firing but now, out the meadow, from the direction in which your sons went!"

"Perhaps the boys found game," said Godfrey, though he turned pale.

"No, this was no sound of hunting I heard," persisted the watchman. "Your sons have been attacked by Indians, or I lose my guess."

In anxiety not to be described the Nimses waited and watched through the long night, often hearing in fancy the footsteps of the missing ones, only to find that hope had deceived them. The night wore on, and still they came not.

With the earliest gray light of dawn, Godfrey Nims, accompanied by a party of friends, all armed, rode out into the meadows to the northwest on the track of the young men. The father's heart was heavy within him, thinking at any moment that he might come upon the mutilated bodies of his sons.

At Frary's bridge and about the pond the party found unmistakable signs of a conflict. The ground was trampled, and Zebediah's hat with two bullet holes in it and stained with blood, lay trodden and torn on the grass. Several cattle, wounded and bleeding, ran eagerly to the white men, seeking help and protection.

But no bodies were found, either there or as far north in the meadow as the party felt it prudent to venture. Driving the wounded cattle before them, the party returned sorrowfully to the stockade with their direful news.

It was plain that Zebediah and John had been taken captive by a band of enemy Indians, probably the same party who had tried to capture Mr. Williams the previous night. In their home was a sorrowful vacancy, even worse than that left by death. Yesterday the two young men were there; brave, strong, smiling. Today they were gone; and no one could tell what tortures and privations they might be suffering.

"Oh if I could only hear from Zebediah, could know where he is!" moaned the young wife in her anguish. "Perchance 't is well we cannot know where they are, or what bearing," said the sorrowful mother, fearing the worst that Indian capture could mean.

How large the band of attacking Indians had been, or whether the same party might not even now be lurking in ambush on the overlooking hills around, watching the settlers' every movement as the cat watches a doomed mouse, ready to fall upon them at any unguarded moment, no one knew But a strong feeling of apprehension settled down over the little outpost.

The October sunlight streamed down as pleasantly as ever. Flocks of wild-geese flew overhead, "honking" as they sped on to the south. The mountains and swamps were resplendent with color. But behind all this beauty lurked a deadly menace to the settlers' fancy. The autumn wind, rustling the dry, bright leaves, and moaning down the huge chimneys, seemed to sigh with foreboding of trouble and anguish, they knew not in what drear forms.

A town-meeting was called in Deerfield October 15th to consider what should be done about the fortifications. So decayed were they that many considered it unwise to waste work upon them, feeling that wholly new palisades were absolutely necessary. Yet how could this small settlement so isolated, so impoverished by constant perils, engage in the labor and expense of building three hundred and twenty rods of new palisades?

In this emergency, the town appointed a committee, consisting of Captain Jonathan Wells *(the boy hero of Turner's Falls, now military commander of Deerfield)*, Lieutenant David Hoyt, Ensign John Sheldon, and Daniel Belding, to confer with Colonel Samuel Partridge of Hatfield. Since the recent death of John Pynchon of Springfield Colonel Partridge had become the leading man in the western section of the colony. The committee was to determine, as the town warrant read, "wheither to fortifi or no and if ye agree to fortifi, in what manar or places."

After this conference, October 27th, Colonel Partridge wrote an urgent letter to Joseph Dudley, governor of the Province of Massachusetts Bay, and to the General Court then assembled, representing forcibly the exposed situation of Deerfield, and the hardships endured by its habitants. He begged that the Court would make some allowance towards rebuilding the stockade. He also asked that the Deerfield people be relieved of their public taxes during the war.

Rev. John Williams had written previously to the governor making the same plea. He also mentioned another hardship now borne by his people: "We have been driven from our houses and home lots into the fort. There but ten house lots in the fort."

This was sadly true. A large part of the people dwelling in the twenty-eight houses outside the fort had moved into it for safety, especially those living north of the stockade. Captain Jonathan Wells had been fortifying his house south of the fort and the inhabitants in that section had therefore a refuge near at hand. But north lay the danger. The eyes of the settlers never ranged across the northern meadows to the blue hills bounding their view without a feeling of apprehension. The fort's northern gate opened out into a vast wilderness, stretching unbroken to Canada, the enemy's abode.

The few settlers who had been tempted to take up land on the fertile, smiling plain where Greenfield now stands, looking down on

Picommegan River *(or "boring river," as the Indian name meant)*, three miles north of the fort, abandoned the houses already built there and took refuge in the stockade, it not being safe to venture so far north even to cultivate their crops. From the north came only danger. The Connecticut River, sweeping along Deerfield's eastern border, and into which flowed their own home stream, the Pocumtuck, offered Indian canoes an easy highway from the far north almost to the settlers' doors.

Earlier in the autumn, Sergeant John Hawks had been given a small plot of land within the fort, on the corner of Mr. Williams's lot, whereon to build. Now the people fell earnestly to work erecting a number of small huts within the fort to shelter those who hurriedly moved into them for protection. Some were even glad to find refuge in small cellars dug in the hillside of the plateau whereon stood the stockade. Benjamin Munn dug such a cellar on the lot of his step-father, Mr. Richards, the schoolmaster, and took refuge there with his family.

Fires could be built in these rude shelters, and beds thrown on the earthen floor. The privations thus endured seemed slight compared to the horrors of possible capture or death at savage hands. The open space within the stockade was cluttered with these temporary refuges. Also, as many of the outsiders as possible were taken under the friendly roofs of those dwelling inside the stockade.

Mrs. Williams had under her roof not only her family of ten, including slaves, but also Jonathan Hoyt, a great friend of Samuel, his sister Sarah, seventeen years old, and a young brother, Benjamin. Esther was made happy by having her friend, Thankful Stebbins, added to their guests, while little Mary Brooks was Eunice's bed-fellow.

The house was literally packed full. The children did not realize the possible dangers ever haunting their parents minds. They were pleased with the novelty and excitement, and the close companionship of playmates, and found the crowded conditions rather agreeable than otherwise.

"I think it's fun to sleep four in a bed," remarked Stephen one morning.

"So do I," said Ben Hoyt, "if Jonathan wouldn't pull the covers off me."

"We will pay him and Sam back, Ben," said Stephen, whispering some sly plot in Ben's ear, whereat Ben laughed, delighted.

Although the Williams house, like all the ten within the fort, seemed already over-full, it was destined to be still further crowded. When Mr. Williams came in to supper the evening of October 20th, his face wore a more relieved, hopeful look than it had borne of late, as he said to wife:

"Good news at last, Eunice. A post has ridden in from the south but now, bringing a letter to Captain Wells from Colonel Partridge, saying that sixteen soldiers from Connecticut are on the road and will probably arrive here tomorrow to reinforce our garrison. Connecticut Colony knows full well that Deerfield is the outpost, the bulwark to the north for all the settlements below, and that our downfall will surely presage their own destruction. So she sends these soldiers to strengthen us."

Truly I am glad," said Mrs. Williams. "But where can the soldiers be quartered, crowded as we are? I see not."

"We must e'en crowd a little closer to make place for them," said Mr. Williams. "I told Captain Wells that we would take two under our roof."

"Two!" exclaimed the wife as she glanced around her cluttered kitchen. The kitchen was already so over-full when all her household were assembled that it was with difficulty the necessary meals for so many were cooked. Spinning, weaving, and other household work was at a standstill for lack of room.

"Yet I think I can manage it," she added in a moment; "for it will certainly give a sense of added protection to have two stout soldiers under our very roof."

"My father," said Sarah Hoyt, "has brought all our bedding into the stockade. Some of it is stored in one of the cellars. I know mother will gladly loan you all you need."

"Then we can put the soldiers in the boys' room, and make up a bed for the boys on the kitchen floor each night," said Mrs. Williams. "We shall be sorely crowded, but that is as naught compared to the feeling of safety I shall have with the Connecticut soldiers added to our garrison."

"I shall not mind sleeping on the kitchen floor," said Samuel. "In truth, I shall rather like it; for since it falls to my lot to rake open the coals and build up the fire every morning, it will be far easier to sleep on the spot than to leap out of bed in the cold and dark and feel my way downstairs "

That is so," said Jonathan. "We boys will be like the gentle-folk of Boston, with a fire in our bedroom."

"And if you and Sam kick Ben and me out of bed now, we shall not have far to fall," said Stephen.

"I wish we girls could have the bed on the kitchen floor," said Esther, moved by the boys' picture of the fun and luxury they were to enjoy.

"O Esther, don't say that," said Thankful Stebbins. "wouldn't sleep on the ground floor for anything! Suppose the Indians should burst in on us right in the middle of the night!"

"Bo-o-oh!" said Esther, shuddering. "I didn't think of that."

"You girls are silly," said Samuel. "How do you suppose the Indians are going to break into our stout new stockade, past our watch, and with all the Connecticut soldiers here, besides our own good guns? I should like to see them do it!"

"Tempt not Providence by rash speech, my son," said the minister. "I pray that God may direct and assist us in these hours of danger, and encourage our hearts to put all our trust in Him."

The boys said no more. But they were on hand the next day when the squad of sixteen soldiers marched in at the fort's south gate. The boys at the minister's eagerly welcomed the two sturdy young men, one from Windsor, one from Hartford, who were assigned to Mr. Williams, and in the long evenings by the fire held much talk with them. Visitors from the outside world were few in this isolated and dangerous outpost, and the boys had much to ask the newcomers about the Connecticut settlements, the Pequot Indians, and kindred matters.

Godfrey Nims was using every effort to redeem his captive sons, if still alive. Nothing was known of their fate since they stepped over the home threshold that fatal night of October 8th, vanishing into the outer darkness. He tried to bring every possible influence in their favor to bear on Governor Dudley. His pastor, Mr. Williams, wrote to the governor m his letter of October 21st:

"The sorrowful parents and distressed widow of the poor captives taken from us request your Excellency that there may be an exchange of prisoners to their release. I know I need not use arguments to move your Excellency's pity and compassion of them."

And Rev. Solomon Stoddard, minister at Northampton, also wrote the governor the next day:

"The father of the two captives belonging to Deerfield, has importunately desired me to write to your Exc'y that you would endeavour the Redemption of his children."

But whatever efforts the governor may have made to redeem the captives were in vain. Nothing was heard of them, and their fate was only matter of sad conjecture.

Later in the winter, the number of soldiers in the garrison at Deerfield was raised to twenty. Because one of the Connecticut soldiers left Mr. Williams's, young John Stoddard, son of the Northampton minister, took his place. This was very pleasing to Mr. Williams and his wife, for they felt that young Stoddard was a most desirable comrade to be living in such close intimacy with their boys.

And so the people of Deerfield passed the autumn in both profound anxiety and great discomfort, huddled as they were within the stockade, and dreading a savage attack which might fall at any moment. Incessant vigilance by day and night was their only safeguard.

# 3

# WEDDING

As weeks and then months passed quietly away, while autumn glided imperceptibly into winter and yet there was no Indian onslaught, the anxious settlers huddled within Deerfield's palisades began to feel more at ease. And life went on, as life does, tarrying not for the fears, the sorrows, or the joys of mortals. There were marriages, births, and deaths within the little settlement. Gradually, absorbed in the happenings and interests of every day, the possibility of Indian attack began to seem more and more remote.

Early on the morning of December 3rd, Widow Elizabeth Smead, who lived south of the stockade, chancing to look out her front window, saw a troop of horsemen riding out the fort's southern gate, down the hill into the highway, and past her house to the south.

The bracing air; the hills purple blue in their naked beauty; the delicate tracery of bare boughs against the clear, cold sky; the wide, uninterrupted view over meadow and field, now that every leaf was gone; made the bright morning absolutely stimulating to youthful blood. Widow Smead herself felt cold and chilly, but the young men galloping by over the frozen ground were laughing and talking in high spirits, their cheeks rosy and eyes bright.

"I wonder whither the boys ride forth so jauntily," she said.

She recognized among the riders young John Sheldon, and his friends John Stebbins and John and Jonathan and Catlin, and she thought, her own grandson, Ebenezer Nims.

"Why, haven't you heard the news, mother?" asked her daughter, Mehitable, wife of Godfrey Nims, who had but just come in. "Young John Sheldon is to be married today to Hannah Chapin of Springfield, and his friends ride down with him as an escort. They all carry their guns, you see. We are to have a blooming young bride among us."

"I wonder at the whole business," said Widow Smead This seems a sorry time for marrying and giving in marriage. I wonder that any young woman in these perilous times is willing to leave the safe settlements down below and venture up here into the wilderness to live. She must be a brave girl."

"Yes, truly, and not only brave but greatly in love with John, too," said Mehitable. "You know the wedding has been postponed, owing to the troublous times. But now the young folks were unwilling to delay longer, and, the parents having consented, the wedding takes place today. I'm glad they have so bright a day."

"Did I see your Ebenezer riding forth with the wedding escort, or did my eyes deceive me?" asked the widow. "Is it possible, Mehitable, that you and his father consented to his going when you have already lost two sons by the Indians?"

"Why, yes, mother," answered Mrs. Nims. "In truth, think his father was not over-pleased to have Ebenezer go, nor was I. But the boy was so urgent that his father finally yielded. Godfrey says it will not do to mew our young men up in the fort, tied to their mothers' apron strings, if we expect them to be manly and courageous. So he said to Ebenezer, 'Go, boy, and take your chances. But be sure to ride in single file through the woods, and keep a watchful eye out for possible ambush by the crafty savages.'

"Ebenezer answered, 'Father, have no fears. The Indians will not catch me, or the pretty bride either, I promise you.' So he has gone. For my part, though apparently there isn't an Indian within two hundred miles of us, I confess I shall feel better when I see the party safely back."

"You may well say that, Mehitable. I shall pray for their safe return," said good Widow Smead. "I trust they will not be caught in a snow storm. Winter is tightening down on us, and bright as the morning seems, this deadly chill in the air means snow, or I am vastly mistaken.

I've piled wood on the fire, and yet I can't keep warm spinning briskly right before it."

"It must be your rheumatism, mother, that makes you over-sensitive to the cold," said Mehitable. "To my mind it is as bright and pleasant a winter's morning as one could ask. But I must home to my little girls, and not stay here idling and gossiping any longer."

Meantime, the young men were riding on in fine spirits along the bridle path that led to Springfield, thirty-three miles to the south. Their horses were fresh and spirited, and the hard frozen ground rang like a pavement under their galloping hoofs. Both men and horses had been so long pent up in the close quarters of the stockade that there was a feeling of wild exhilaration in again sallying forth into the outside world.

"Truly, John," said Ebenezer Nims, "'t was vastly kind of you to bethink yourself of marrying just now. It gives us all a little change."

"Yes, that is so," said John Catlin. "A wedding and a pretty new face brought in among us will brighten matters in the old fort not a little."

"And 't is so reviving to get outside again and ride briskly off at a good pace," said John Stebbins. "As Eben says, we are all obliged to you, John."

"I'm sure you're all most welcome," said the radiant bridegroom, "though, to tell the truth, I am marrying rather for my own sake than to oblige my neighbors."

"Your Hannah must be as brave as she is pretty, John," said Joseph Catlin. "Few are the maidens that would be tempted to leave the safety of Springfield and cast in their lot with our exposed settlement, especially now, when there have been so many rumors of Indian attack."

"Her mother joked her when Hannah was making her wedding pelisse," said John. "She charged her to make it thick and warm, for she might need it were she carried off to Canada by the Indians. But Hannah cared not. Her mind was made up, and neither joking nor warning was going to turn her."

John did not tell his comrades that in a moment of tender confidence Hannah had blushingly whispered, "Can I not take the same risks you do, John? What would life be worth to me were you captured or slain and I left behind alone? "I am like Naomi, John, —where thou goest I will go."

The cavalcade had now reached Indian Bridge, in the south meadow.

"This is the place where the Indians ambushed my father and Joseph Barnard and the others," said Ebenezer Nims.

"Yes, and had not your father taken Barnard up on his horse, Barnard would have lost his scalp in a minute more," said John Catlin.

"That reminds me," said John Sheldon. "It will be more prudent now for us to ride in single file. Though no Indians are about, it is wise to take all due precautions. The bridle path narrows soon, and presently we shall be in the forest going up the Long Hill."

"'Tis not such good-fellowship, but no doubt it is safer," said Jonathan Catlin, as he reined back his horse and dropped behind John, his example followed by the other riders.

The early settlers had not been long in learning the wisdom of following the Indian plan, in either walking riding through the forest, of going in single file, about a rod apart. The party were thus not so easily caught in ambush, and if one were shot, the rest had a chance to take refuge behind trees.

The young riders made such good speed that they trotted into the palisade gate at Northampton by noon. Here they crossed the Connecticut by ferry, and then stopped to rest and bait their horses at the ordinary kept by Joseph Kellogg, the venerable ferryman.

Soon they rode on again, through the Great Meadow, into Hadley s north gate. Here they delayed a short time to exchange news and friendly greetings with various acquaintances, for the relations between the Valley settlements were close. Not only were there many ties of blood and intermarriage, but the youths of the lower towns were often obliged to take their turn at serving on the garrisons sent up from below to guard Deerfield, the frontier outpost of all the settlements.

"All mankind loves a lover," and the good folks of Hadley were no exception. They admired the spirit of Hannah Chapin, and sped young Sheldon on his way with their warmest good wishes.

Japhet Chapin, Hannah's father, lived near the northern boundary of Springfield, in the section known by its Indian name Scanunganunk, where the path to Springfield crossed the Chicopee River, near the island. The young men reached his house that afternoon without difficulty, safe and sound, and in the best of spirits.

The next morning dawned gray and chilly, with an ominous feeling of snow in the air.

"I told you so. I knew that ache in my bones wasn't for nothing," the Widow Smead was able to say triumphantly, as she viewed the threatening sky from her window. "I trust this dark day and coming storm bode no ill to the to the young bride."

A wedding always arouses sympathetic interest, and in the dearth of events, and the monotony of life within Deerfield stockade, everyone felt the most intense concern in the welfare of the young bride and groom. They watched the clouds with almost personal anxiety, hoping the coming storm might not block and delay the homeward journey.

Perhaps this strong tide of human sympathy availed to hold the storm back. At all events, it was late in the afternoon when the first scattering snowflakes began to straggle reluctantly down, slowly thickening until the early darkness fell amid a whirling, blinding maze of whiteness.

"If all has gone well with them, we may expect our young folks home ere long," said John Sheldon, senior, as he came in, stamping off the snow.

"'T is a wonderful mercy the storm has held off so long," said his wife, as she helped brush away the snow covering her husband. "It cannot block their way now, for they must be too near home."

She opened the door, peering out into the storm.

"I declare, John, here they are now, I do believe."

Up to the door of her future home rode young Mistress Hannah Sheldon on the pillion behind her husband. She clasped his waist tightly with her encircling arms, white and shaggy with the driving storm. Heartily was she welcomed by her new father and mother.

"Blessings on your pretty face," said Mr. Sheldon as he lifted down his new daughter from the saddle and caught a glimpse of her shy, sweet face in the light streaming out the open door.

"Welcome, my daughter," said Mrs. Sheldon warmly, thinking of the time, so long ago, when she, a bride of only fifteen summers, had gone to dwell at her father-in-law's in Northampton.

In spite of the storm, some of the neighbors and young people had assembled at Mr. Sheldon's to welcome home the bride. Mr. Williams offered a fervent prayer, invoking God's blessing on the union. Cake and wine were passed, for, as Mrs. Sheldon said,—

"We don't have a wedding every day, and, even though times are hard and dark, I think it only fitting and decent to give our children a good send-off."

"You are right, good Mrs. Sheldon," said Mr. Williams the cockles of his heart warmed a little by the wine. "It has ever been the custom from the most ancient times to make a wedding a season of gladness, festivity, and merry-making. So it is seemly for us to do, with all due regard to Christian propriety."

Several staves of a psalm were sung, as was customary at weddings. And then Jonathan Catlin was urged to lead off in the "Forefathers' Song," so well known to all, that after Jonathan's clear tenor voice had once started it, many joined in. The verses were sung to rather a rollicking and the heart of the night-watch pacing up and down in the storm outside was cheered within him by the sounds of merriment from the Sheldon house.

This was the song, in part:

"When the spring opens we then take the hoe
And make the ground ready to plant and to sow:
Our corn being planted and seed being sown,
The worms destroy much before it is grown:
And when it is growing, some spoil there is made
By birds and by squirrels that pluck up the blade:
And when it is come to full corn in the ear,
It is often destroyed by raccoon and by deer.

"And now, too, our garments begin to grow thin,
And wool is much wanted to card and to spin:
If we can get a garment to cover without,
Our other in-garments are clout upon clout:
Our clothes we brought with us are apt to be torn,
They need to be clouted soon after they're worn.
But clouting our garments, they hinder us nothing,
Clouts double are warmer than single whole clothing.

For pottage and puddings and custards and pies,
Our pumpkins and parsnips are common supplies.
We have pumpkins at morning and pumpkins at noon,
If it were not for pumpkins we should be undone.
If barley be wanting to make into malt,
We must be contented and think it no fault:

For we can make liquor to sweeten our lips,
With pumpkins and parsnips and walnut-tree chips."

At the close of this song, Mr. Williams, looking around on the smiling young faces, improved the occasion by saying:

"To sing this song is not mere idle merry-making, for it well illustrates the hardships and self-denial of our forefathers in the first settlement of this colony, and teaches us to be thankful for the many mercies which we are now privileged to enjoy."

When the guests left at last, each was given a large piece of the wedding cake, carefully wrapped in paper, to take home.

Ebenezer Nims felt it necessary to see fair Sarah Hoyt home that night, although she only went to her temporary home at Mr. Williams's, near by. As he handed her the parcel of cake in parting, he said laughingly:

"You know, Sarah, if you put a bit of that bride's cake under your pillow tonight, whatever you dream on it will certainly come true. Be sure to dream of me, Sallie."

"Don't be foolish, Eben," said Sarah, dashing into the house, and hastily closing the door, lest even in the dark Ebenezer spy her blushes and think she "cared."

# 4

# A NEW ARRIVAL

THE winter proved unusually severe, storm following storm until
a great depth of snow covered the ground. One fine day in January, when the sun shone dazzlingly on the pure white snow covering
meadows and pine-clad mountains; when every breath of the crisp,
pure air seemed to inspire one to action and confidence; Martin Kellogg chanced to meet one of his neighbors at the north end, David
Hoyt. Hoyt was variously called Deacon or Lieutenant Hoyt, for he
filled both offices.

"Deacon," said Martin, "does not this fine, seasonable weather make
you restive, cooped up here in the stockade? For my part, I long to
move back again under my own roof-tree, and even my wife suffers
so sorely from the inconveniences we must perforce endure here that
she is willing at last to venture back to her own house."

"Yes," said Deacon Hoyt. "It is the same with my wife. When I
first broached the idea of moving back home, she would not hear a
word of it. But now, as time goes on, and all is quiet, she has grown
as anxious to return as I. We feel, not only our own inconveniences,
but also those suffered by our kind neighbors, into whose houses we
have been so hospitably taken. No matter how willingly borne, the
hardships are great for them. My wife feels especially that good Mrs.

Williams, our pastor's wife, should be relieved from further care of our children."

"We feel the same," said Kellogg. "All is quiet and has been, and there seems little likelihood of our being at-tacked this winter, especially with the unusual depth of snow now on the ground."

"Unless Satan himself helps them, I see not how it is humanly possible for the Indians to traverse the two hundred miles of wilderness between us and Canada in such depth of snow," said the deacon. "You know the old Indian fighters among us always say, 'No fear of Indians till the leaves put forth in the spring. Then look out for them.' I think it perfectly safe for the present outside the stockade. I am now on my way, as you see, with a foot-stove full of live coals to start a blazing fire on our hearthstone, that the chill may be taken off the house, ere we move out home tomorrow."

"I will do the same," said Kellogg.

Most of the other families from outside soon followed the example of Deacon Hoyt arid Martin Kellogg. Their pastor, Mr. Williams, could not share the hopeful feeling pervading his flock, and strongly urged them to postpone such action.

"It seems to me rash, almost a direct tempting of Providence, for you thus needlessly to expose yourselves," he said. "True, we must all suffer some inconvenience, huddled in together as we are; but what is that, compared to one's life?"

"Parson Williams, if I thought for one moment that the lives of my wife and children were endangered, I would be the last one to make this move," replied Kellogg. "But it seems to me entirely safe, as it does to Deacon Hoyt, John Stebbins, and others of the dwellers at the north end."

"Daniel Belding does not follow your example," said Mr. Williams. "Like a wise man, he tarries within the palisades."

"In truth, that is little to be wondered at," said Kellogg. "The burnt child dreads the fire. Had the rest of us undergone the sorrowful experiences that he and Mrs. Belding have suffered, I dare say we should be more timorous."

Daniel Belding had married Hepzibah, widow of Thomas Wells. Both she and her husband had undergone terrible suffering at the hands of Indians in times sufficiently recent to be vividly remembered. In 1693 the house of the Widow Wells, near the extreme north end of Deer-field, was attacked by a party of savages. Two of her daughters were scalped, and one was killed. In 1696, Daniel Belding's house had been attacked by sixteen French Mohawks. His wife, two sons, and a daughter were slain. Another son and daughter were badly wounded, and Belding himself, with his oldest son and a daughter of thirteen were carried off into captivity. At Fort Oso, in Canada, Mr. Belding was forced to run the gantlet, but, as history tells us, "being a nimble or light-footed man, received few blows, save at first setting out." After living ten months in Canada as captives, Mr. Belding and his children were redeemed through the efforts of the Schuylers of Albany, and came home.

In 1699 Daniel Belding had married the Widow Wells. She was the same Hepzibah Wells who when she came a proud young bride to Hadley was twice fined in Northampton Court for undue finery in dress. Time and sad experiences had chilled the high spirit of her youth. It was not strange that she and her present husband shrank from exposing themselves to any possible risk of danger from Indians.

The next event of general interest in Deerfield can best be told in the words of Eunice Williams. On the morning of January 15th, the little girl ran across the stockade and past the meeting-house, following the footpath trampled in the snow as it wound among the various small temporary houses or huts built to shelter the settlers from outside. These huts almost filled what had been the training field in the stockade's centre. She ran breathlessly into the house of Godfrey Nims, eager to be the first to tell her great news to her girl friends, Mehitable and Mary Nims.

As she entered the room, Mrs. Nims, smiling, said:

"Here comes little Eunice, with great news for us, I fancy."

"Yes, indeed, Mrs. Nims," panted the child. "I have a little new sister, a real baby sister of my own! She came in the night last night. Esther says that doubtless good Mrs. Sheldon brought her, or perchance Mrs. Frary, for they were both there all night with my mother, Esther says. Mrs. Carter is there now."

"That is great news, indeed, Eunice," said Mrs. Nims. "I must brew a bowl of posset and take over to your mother, with a strengthening cordial that I have, of wondrous virtue. I am very glad for her, and for you all."

"I guess you're glad, Eunice," said little Mary Nims. "I wish I were you. I wish I had a little baby sister."

"I would rather have a baby brother," said Mehitable. "He wouldn't tease me as Henry docs."

"Pshaw, that's nothing," said Henry Nims, a boy of twelve, with roguish black eyes. "Boys always lease their sisters. They can't help it; girls are so easily teased. Now boys don't care."

"You're bigger and older than we are. That's the reason you don't care what we say to you," said Mehitable.

"Tut, tut, children. Don't dispute. You mustn't mind Henry, Mehitable," said the mother. "Often he is only joking, when he plays his pranks. He doesn't mean to be rough. What will the new sister's name be, Eunice?"

"Jerusha, after our baby sister that died. She's going to be baptized next Sunday."

"Yes, I supposed so," said Mrs. Nims.

"I must go home now to hold my baby sister," said Eunice. "Mrs. Carter said I might, if I would be very careful. You ought to see her dear little hands and feet. They are not much bigger than a kitten's."

"Can't we go right over now and see the baby, mother?" asked Mary and Mehitable in one breath.

"No. You must wait a few days. I fancy Mrs. Williams has quite as much disturbance as is good for her with her own family just now."

"Mrs. Frary has taken John and Warham home to stay with her for a few days," said Eunice, "and Mrs. Catlin asked the big boys to her house, and John Stoddard and the other soldier take their meals over at Benoni Stebbins's, only coming home to sleep. So there are only Esther and I at home now. It seems so strange to have such a small family."

Crowded as Deerfield homes were, its people could always crowd themselves a little closer to aid a neighbor. Indeed, neighborly help was the chief reliance in illness. There was no doctor in Deerfield, the nearest being Dr. Thomas Hastings of Hatfield. Persons seriously ill were often taken to Hatfield or to Connecticut for medical treatment. Captain Jonathan Wells, after his miraculous escape from the battle of Turner's Falls, was carried to Hartford for cure, remaining some months, his expenses being shared by the General Court and the town of Hadley. And Mrs. Hepzibah Wells took her two surviving daughters to Windsor, Connecticut, for treatment, after they were scalped by the Indians in 1693.

Drug stores were unknown in all the settlements. The doctors imported a few drugs from England. But in every attic hung great bunches of dried herbs and roots, nature's own simples: thoroughwort, saffron, tansy, wormwood, sage, rue, dandelion, burdock, coltsfoot, catnip, mint, and the like. The use of many of these plants had been learned from the Indians. It was part of the house-mother's duties to be skilled in the use of these home remedies and in nursing, and the older women especially were often experts in medicine.

So the neighboring women watched with, nursed, and doctored one another in sickness, with infinite warmth of loving-kindness and neighborly good-feeling. Fortunately illness was rare in those days of plain living, simple fare, and hardy toil.

The following Sunday was a zero day, with a piercing northwest wind that seemed to penetrate even to the marrow of the bones. As big logs as the boys could draw into the kitchen on sleds were stacked up in the huge fireplaces, making great roaring fires that burned and flushed people's faces, while ever, from the rear of the room, a cold draft sucked in towards the fireplace; a draft from which even the settle's high back could not protect the shoulders.

Thankful Stebbins sat huddled up in the warmest corner of the settle before the fire in her father's home outside the stockade, listening to the wind as it roared down the chimney. The morning's work was done and everyone was ready for meeting. Thankful was supposed to be studying her catechism, but evidently her mind wandered, for presently she said:

"Bo-o-oh! Do hear that wind! I am cold sitting here. We shall freeze in church today, I know. I wish Mr. Williams would not preach such long sermons. I wish—" here she hesitated and cast a timid glance at her mother, for well she knew this was a daring venture, "I wish I need not go to church today."

"Thankful!" exclaimed her mother, "what ails you, child? Do you feel ill?"

"No, mother, but 't is so terribly cold."

"I am surprised, Thankful," said her mother, "that a child of mine should even think of staying at home from divine service when perfectly well for such a trifling excuse as that."

"It takes more than a snap of cold weather to keep your true New Englanders at home from meeting," said Mr. Stebbins. "I want my children, Thankful, to be sturdy and reliable, and worthy of their old Puritan ancestors. They went to mill or to meeting, hot or cold. If anything was to be done, they simply went ahead and did it, no matter what effort it cost. Let us hear no more about staying at home from meeting. Nor do I like to hear you criticise good Mr. Williams's sermons. He is a right New England Christian, a soul-searching preacher, and if he has the gift of continuance, 't is something to glory in, not to complain of."

Thankful looked abashed and downcast. Then her mother said:

"You have forgotten, I guess, that Mr. Williams's newborn babe is to be baptized today."

Thankful's face brightened. Then she loitered again, saying:

"But perhaps they will not take the little new baby out today, it is so cold."

"Every babe must be baptized the first Sunday after its birth, and that you know full well, Thankful," said her mother. "Is it likely our good Parson Williams would be the first to break this godly custom? But hasten, child, for yonder go the Brookses and Mr. and Mrs. Belding and Mary Wells. We shall be the last comers, I fear."

The Beldings, moved by their neighbors' example, had lately ventured to return to their own home.

Samuel had already filled his mother's tin foot-stove with hot coals, and was banking up the fire with ashes, that it might be safely kept until the family's return.

"Hasten, Thankful," said her mother. "The Hoyts and the Kelloggs are already walking past. We shall be late, which is not seemly."

Thankful hastened to tie on her warm hood and long cloak, and the Stebbinses joined the family processions, pouring along the settlement's one street, all headed for the meeting-house. Every member of every family was there, unless ill, down to the smallest toddlers and the infants in arms.

The meeting-house, a square, two-story building with a pyramidal roof rising to a point in the centre, surmounted by a whirling weathercock, stood in the open space near the centre of the stockade.

Within, wooden benches without cushions were ranged each side the main aisle running from the door to the high pulpit, rising under its over-hanging sounding-board. There was no paint, gilding, or ornament. Ceiling, walls, floor, and benches were alike made of unpainted boards.

The women and girls occupied the benches on one side of the building, the men and boys those on the other. Deacon Hoyt and Deacon Sheldon sat with dignity becoming their office in the deacons' seat beneath the high pulpit, facing the congregation.

It could hardly be wondered at that Thankful had objected to attending service on account of the cold. The building was absolutely unheated, and its icy chill made the blood stagnate.

"It's ever so much colder here than it is outdoors," whispered Joseph Kellogg to Stephen Williams, who sat next him on the cold bench, shivering and beginning to clap his feet together.

Stephen only nodded his head in assent. He was the minister's son, and, whatever happened, must not commit the sin of whispering in meeting, especially as he chanced to notice Deacon Hoyt looking sternly down at Joseph.

The breath of the congregation rose in foglike clouds, adding a still thicker coating to the dense white frost thickly covering the small windows. The children blew on their mittens to warm their fingers, and then tucked their hands under cloaks, to cherish the faint feeling of warmth thus gained as long as possible.

More than one mother, like Mrs. Stebbins, kindly pushed her foot-stove along to warm a little daughter's feet. A foot-stove was such a luxury! But only women must be thus pampered. It would have been considered unmanly for men and boys thus to coddle themselves.

The congregation sat it out bravely, though as the long sermon went on, even the men were forced to rap their feet briskly together to restore chilled circulation. The rapping and stamping of boots echoed through the icy atmosphere with no little noise. But Mr. Williams well understood the necessity of the case, and that no disrespect was intended. He merely raised his voice, and calmly proceeded with his "ninthly," "tenthly," and so on. He himself wore while preaching a skull cap, a heavy cloak, and woollen mittens.

The children all forgot their discomfort when, at the proper time, Mr. Williams came down from the pulpit, saying that an infant would now be presented for baptism. A wave of interest went over the whole congregation, indeed, for any variation in the usual routine was enlivening. And the women had heard that Mrs. Stoddard, wife of the Northampton minister, had sent up by her son John an embroidered cap and blanket for the baby's christening more beautiful than aught e'er seen before in Deerfield. The smaller children were allowed to stand up on the benches for a better view of the ceremony.

Esther Williams had been allowed to take her baby sister in for baptism. She was a proud and happy little girl, realizing her own importance, and how some of her mates envied her, as she walked up the aisle bearing in her arms what looked like a small bundle of blankets, so carefully was the three-day-old baby wrapped from even a breath of outer air. Water had been brought over from Parson Williams's house just before the baby's advent, for if suffered to stand long in the meeting-house it would soon have been frozen.

Arrived before the pulpit, Esther laid back the folds of blanket, exposing to view the tiny pink face, and little head in its close white cap. Such an atom of humanity the baby looked, and yet she was a soul beginning life's pilgrimage.

Mr. Williams sprinkled her face with water, saying impressively, "Jerusha, I baptize thee in the name of the Father, and the Son, and the Holy Ghost. Amen. Let us pray."

All stood reverently, as Mr. Williams prayed long and fervently for God's blessing on the little one.

At baptisms the children always listened eagerly to see if the baby cried when the cold water fell on its face. Lusty shouts were sometimes heard from the babies, but not today. This little one made no outcry.

"I believe Jerusha knew she was a minister's baby," said little Eunice after church. "She never cried once when father sprinkled her face. I was just as proud of her as I could be."

"So was I," said Esther. "And Joanna Kellogg said her cap was the finest wrought baby's cap she ever saw."

This talk was in the mother's bedroom, downstairs, opening out of the kitchen and living-room. Here the girls had come, on reaching home from meeting, to tell mother all about the baptism. Their father had entered, unnoticed, behind them.

"My daughters," he said, "have a care lest ye bring down the frowns of God upon us by your foolish prating and worldly pride, above all on the Sabbath. 'T was thought by many grave and solid persons among us that King Philip's War was sent upon our colonies as a direct punishment for the light-mindedness and sins in dress of some of the lighter sort. Pride goeth before a fall, and a haughty spirit before destruction, says Solomon."

"The girls meant no harm, father," said Mrs. Williams. "Their love for their baby sister makes them talk somewhat foolishly, as young folks will. We will hope, my daughters," she said, with a loving smile at the two little girls, "that our precious little one may grow up to be a good Christian woman, and a helper in the world. That is the best we can ask for her."

"Come out to luncheon now, children," said Mr. Williams. "We must make ready to return to the afternoon service."

During the short nooning a cold luncheon was eaten, and people warmed themselves, preparatory to returning to the meeting-house for the second service. Often, at the close of his morning's discourse, Mr. Williams announced:

"With the divine permission, this subject will be continued in the afternoon."

When the afternoon service was over, Parthena, who with Frank had attended both services sitting with Mr. Sheldon's "Coffee" and the other slaves in the "negroes' pew" in one corner of the gallery, hastened to prepare a hot supper. It was eaten with hearty appetite, and then the children sitting on blocks in the inglenook, or on the settle, luxuriated in the warm glow of the fire. They felt happy and relieved. Sunday was almost over. They had done their duty; now they could be comfortable.

The fireplace shone out cheerfully, glistening in the bright pewter on the dresser's shelves. The ears of corn, crook-necked squashes, flitches of bacon, and the like, hanging from the great beams that ran across the kitchen's ceiling, cast fantastic shadows in the dancing firelight, that made Eunice whisper to Stephen:

"See all the little black imps dancing on the ceiling!"

Over the mantel hung a candle in a tin candlestick with a long back. But Mr. Williams, who was trying to read "Flavell on Fear," one of his much prized books, received more light on its pages from the high blazing fire than from the candle.

Samuel, who had been over to Thomas French's on an errand, now came in, stamping his feet, and whitened all over with snow.

"What! Is it snowing again?" asked his father.

"Yes, father. I ne'er saw it fall faster. If it keeps on this winter as it has begun, we stand a chance of being buried up here in Deerfield. Benoni Stebbins says he noticed yesterday that the snow was drifted nearly to the top of the palisades on the north side."

"The deep falling snow is another of God's mercies vouchsafed us," said Mr. Williams, "for certainly the enemy can never come in upon us from Canada through such a wondrous depth of snow as we have this winter."

This comfortable belief was shared by all the settlers.

# 5

# A WARNING OMEN

THE end of February was now drawing near. One night, when the Catlins, like most of the Deerfield people, were quietly abed and asleep, and when intense stillness brooded over the sleeping settlement, Ruth Catlin suddenly wakened, with a vague feeling of apprehension. It seemed to her that she heard the sound of many footsteps. She sat up, straining her ears to listen. Yes, it was true. She plainly heard the footsteps of a multitude trampling around the outside of the fort!

Terrified beyond measure, she leaped from bed, throwing a blanket around her, and ran down to the door of her parents' room, knocking and calling wildly.

"What is the matter, Ruth?" asked her mother, while the tired father hardly wakened.

"I hear many footsteps. I fear the Indians have comer," cried Ruth, her heart beating so tumultuously that she could no longer distinguish its thump from the sound of the footsteps.

Mrs. Catlin sprang up to listen, while the father was now also aroused. Presently he said:

"I hear naught. All seems quiet as the grave. Do you hear any sound, Mary?"

"No, I hear not a sound," said his wife. "You must have had a bad dream, Ruth."

"No, mother, I certainly heard the sound of many footsteps trampling about the palisades as plainly as I hear your voice now. I knew it was Indians. It wakened me from a sound sleep."

"'Twas doubtless a dream," said her mother. "Go to bed, child, and think no more of it. You will take cold, standing shivering there. Besides, I fear you will waken the little girls, and terrify them here, away from their parents."

The Catlins had taken home temporarily their three pretty little grand-daughters, children of their oldest daughter, Mary, who had married Thomas French, and lived next door, because to the Frenches had lately been born a baby boy.

Ruth knew she must not waken the children, who slept in her room, and so she tiptoed cautiously back to her bed, cheered and comforted by having unburdened her fears to father and mother.

Ah, what a blessed refuge is that! Truly did Auerbach say:

"So long as we can say 'father' and 'mother' there is something to love in the world which bears one in its arms; it is only when the parents are gone that one is set down on the hard ground."

Poor Ruth was soon to be "set down on the hard ground," though now she was mercifully shielded from knowledge of coming events. At this moment her father was not feeling wholly in loving mood towards her.

"It is a vexing thing to be wakened from one's first hard sleep for nothing but a silly girl's fancies," he grumbled, after Ruth had gone. "If Ruth were younger, I vow I should be tempted to trounce her smartly."

"You know Ruth is not very strong," said her mother, "and doubtless that makes her more fearful and fanciful. We must be patient with her. Go to sleep and try to forget it, John."

"Easier said than done when one has been so joustled and started up out of a sound sleep," said Mr. Catlin.

The next morning her younger brother John, hearing of Ruth's midnight alarm, teased her not a little.

"So, Mistress Ruth," he said, "you were going to have the Indians in upon us forthwith. What a silly goose you were, running about in the night, cackling and disturbing the whole house just for a dream!"

"It was no dream," said Ruth, with spirit, though she still looked pale. "I don't care what you say. I don't know what it was, or what caused the noise; but I do know I heard it, and a most awesome sound it was.

I cannot throw off the feeling of it yet. And when I went over to Mrs. Carter's for milk this morning she spoke of hearing the same sound."

"Mrs. Carter is always imagining something," said John. "Did you suppose, Ruth, an enemy could be marching in upon us like that, unheard by our watchman, who paces the street all night, ready to fire his gun in signal of alarm at the first suspicious appearance? Next time you had best keep your wits about you, Ruth, and not cry out till you are hurt."

"You may laugh all you please, John," said Ruth, "I know what I heard. Had you chanced to hear those footsteps too, you would sing another song."

"Footsteps!" said John, contemptuously. But later in the morning Mr. Catlin came in looking seriously disturbed. He nodded to his wife, motioning her to step into their bedroom.

"What is it, John?" asked his wife, anxiously.

"Don't let the children hear of it," said the husband, in hushed tone. "It seems that strange disturbance last night was not wholly in our Ruth's fancy, after all. The same sound was plainly heard by Mr. Williams and his wife, by Benoni Stebbins and Deacon Sheldon and others, exactly as Ruth described it. Benoni says he could have taken his oath that a large army was marching around our fort, though silently, with no sound but this of their trampling feet. Early this morning he and our son-in-law, Thomas French, were up and out, looking over the palisades. There was not a track of human foot in the deep snow that lies all around them; only the straggling marks left by the wolves ever prowling about."

"It seems most ominous," said Mrs. Catlin, with pale face. "What does Mr. Williams advise?"

"He has asked the men of the settlement to meet with him this afternoon to consider what this omen portends. But keep the whole matter from Ruth and the other children as long as possible. It will only frighten them; I trust for naught."

"I pray so, with all my heart," said Mrs. Catlin, assuming as cheerful a face as possible, to return to her family and her work.

Mr. Williams, who as pastor of this little flock afar in the wilderness had been unable to overcome his heavy sense of responsibility and anxious foreboding, considered these mysterious sounds, which had cost him his night's sleep, an alarming portent.

"'Tis well known to you all," he said to the men assembled in council, "that the horrors of King Philip's War were foretold by many significant omens. During an eclipse of the moon, the perfect form of an Indian scalp was seen imprinted on it. An Indian bow appeared in the sky. The wind was noticed to sound like the whistling of bullets, and several reliable persons reported hearing invisible troops of horses galloping through the air. Even the wolves howled in a boding manner."

"It has seemed to me that the wolves have howled more drearily than usual around our fort of late," said Thomas French.

"This mysterious noise, heard by many of us last night, plainly made by no earthly footsteps, is to my mind clearly a direct warning from God of coming danger, though I know not from what source to look for danger now," said Mr. Williams. "But it behooves us to bestir ourselves to redouble our vigilance, and above all, to strive to appease the anger of God by earnest professions of humiliation. I will therefore appoint day after tomorrow—that due notice may reach all—as a day of fasting, humiliation, and prayer. We will ask God either to spare us, and save us from the hands of our enemies, or to prepare us to honor and sanctify Him in whatsoever way He shall come forth to us."

Two services were held on the fast day thus appointed, as generally attended by all the people as were the regular Sunday services. Work was suspended and a rigid fast observed until sundown.

In the morning Mr. Williams preached from Genesis, thirty-second chapter, tenth and eleventh verses: "I am not worthy of the least of all the mercies, and of all the truth, which thou hast shewed unto thy servant. . . . Deliver me, I pray thee, from the hand of my brother, from the hand of Esau: for I fear him, lest he will come and smite me, and the mother with the children."

In the afternoon his text was from Genesis, thirty-second chapter, twenty-sixth verse: "And he said, Let me go, for the day breaketh: and he said, I will not let thee go, except thou bless me."

With earnestness that rose to eloquence, the pastor, to quote his own words, "spread the causes of fear relating to ourselves or families before God." While he implored God to spare his people, to accept their penitence and humiliation, he entreated his flock to place all their trust in God, and no matter what might befall them, in every condition to be always following God in unquestioning faith.

The people went home greatly impressed by their minister's fervor, and the fearful among them much comforted and strengthened by the services.

Only a few days after the fast came the last day of February. The sun already seemed to shine more warmly, with something of spring-like softness. Ruth Catlin called joyously out her open window, as she was upstairs making her bed, to Sarah Hoyt, who was passing below:

"Sarah, what do you think? I heard the first robin this morning!"

"Are you sure?" asked Sarah.

"Yes, indeed, I am, for I saw him too, bright little red-breast, perched up in one of our apple trees."

"I'm so glad," said Sarah. "That must mean that spring is coming right along."

"I hope so, for I never was so tired of winter in my life," said Ruth.

All the Deerfield settlers shared the cheerful feeling which comes in New England with the knowledge that the long, cold winter months are a thing of the past, and that soon spring bloom and summer delights may be again expected.

"We shall be out working in our fields and meadows again, before many weeks," said Mr. Belding to Deacon Hoyt. "I am looking over my seeds now, and getting tools ready."

"Yes, God willing," said the deacon. "I should rejoice in our letting out again, after our long, close imprisonment this winter, but for the dread I cannot help feeling that the Indians may come in upon us when the leaves are out."

"We must, of course, go well guarded to our work," said Mr. Belding. "In my opinion, it would be wise to keep scouts ever out to the north, that the enemy may have no chance to come down upon us unprepared. Our new stockade is stout and strong, and if warned in season, I think we shall have no trouble in defending ourselves and repulsing the foe."

"At all events, we may feel safe for the present, with this great body of snow on the ground," said the deacon, "though often I ponder what that ominous warning portended. It behooves us to walk straightly, lest we bring down the wrath of God upon us."

The sunset that night was followed by a ruddy afterglow that illumined the whole sky above the western mountains with a clear shining red, deepening as the night shadows began to fall from the east into a thicker, darker tinge. The glittering crust on the wild waste of snow covering field and meadow outside the palisade, and the icy surface of the Pocumtuck, gleamed red in the reflected glow, in which the new moon hung low over the mountains.

Mrs. Williams, who, though far from strong, was now able to be about the house somewhat, came to the front door, her baby in her arms, to call in the children who were playing outside. Stephen was tugging manfully, drawing Eunice and little John and Warham on a rude sled which he had made himself, with some help from Sam.

"Come in now," called Mrs. Williams's pleasant voice. "The darkness will soon fall, and you children must all make ready for supper."

"Oh, mother," cried Eunice, "cannot we stay out just a little longer? There is such a nice crust, and Stephen is playing he is the post, travelling down to the Bay, and we are his passengers going with him."

"No. Come in now," said the motherly voice, "and tomorrow you can play again, if you and Stephen do your tasks faithfully first."

"I would I could go outside the palisade to-morrow," said Stephen, as he obeyed his mother, and drew his passengers up to the doorstone. "The snow within here has been so trampled and trodden down that it is hard to find a smooth place. But outside the stockade it is hard and smooth, and glistens like ice. I could easily go over even as far as the river."

"That is not to be thought of for a moment, Stephen," said his mother, closing the door behind the children, both rosy cheeked and hungry after their joyous play outdoors.

Parthena, who was getting supper in the back kitchen, said to her mistress, as she brought in a huge dish of steaming hot samp and set it on the table, where stood a pile of pewter porringers, a pewter tankard of milk, and Mrs. Williams's silver cup:

"Mistress Williams, I'm scared. Just look out that back window. The new moon looks as if it were wading in blood, and the sky, the snow,—all is covered with blood."

"'Tis but the afterglow, Parthena. Perchance its unusual brightness betokens spring weather," said Mrs. Williams. "Say no more of such direful fancies. I would not like the children to hear such talk!"

Parthena shook her head gloomily. But John and War-ham here came out into the back kitchen, for they loved Parthena, who, like all negroes, doted on children. Many was the nice titbit Parthena slipped into her darlings' hands.

"Bless their sweet souls," she said. "Of course Parthena wouldn't frighten her darlings, would she, pet?" chucking Warham under the chin as she spoke.

"No, of course not," said Warham.

But later Parthena cast another glance out the western window at the dusky red sky now fading into gloom, where the stars were coming solemnly forth, one by one, and said to herself:

"Mistress may say what she pleases. That bloody sky means bloody doings."

After supper the family settled down to the usual quiet home occupations, and went peacefully to bed at an early hour. Darkness and silence fell upon this remote little settlement.

The watchman on guard that night paced up and down the stockade's bounds nearly through the night. The hardest time for a watchman was the last hour or two before dawn. Feeling that the night was practically over, the strain of vigilance was then half-unconsciously relaxed, and therefore the fatigue of the long night's walk was felt more sensibly.

Tired with his weary walking to and fro all night, trying hard to shake off the deadly drowsiness threatening to close his heavy eyes even as he still dragged himself up and down, the watchman chanced to hear in a house he was passing a mother softly crooning a lullaby to quiet a sick child. He stood still, leaning heavily against the window-sill to listen. Soothed by the brooding song, and by a sound, faintly heard, as of the wind coming in fitful gusts from the north, slumber stole upon him unawares.

Another moment, as it seemed, and he found himself seized, surrounded by a crowd of hideous painted Indians! It is a dreadful dream, he thinks, as he stares, wild-eyed, at his fierce assailants. Then too late he realized the terrible truth. Deerfield had been surprised and taken by savages!

Half awake as he was, he managed to fire his gun once, crying in tones half stifled by sinewy red hands over his mouth:

"Arm! Arm!"

Then his gun was wrenched from his bewildered grasp, and he was bound, a helpless captive moaning, as he heard on all sides shots and groans and vain cries for help:

"Oh, had I not slept! Had I not slept! God, forgive me if Thou canst! Woe, woe is me for my faithlessness. Woe, woe!"

# 6

# THE BLOW FALLS

VAUDREUIL, French Governor of Canada, to hold fast his allies, the Abenaki Indians, and keep their good-will, as well as to deal a telling blow upon the English, had sent an army from Canada to attack Deerfield and murder in cold blood its defenseless people. The force numbered two hundred French, and a hundred and forty Indians, part of them French Mohawks, as those Mohawks were called who had been converted, partly civilized by the Jesuit missionaries, and settled in a colony at Caghnawaga, near Montreal. Part were Abenakis, and part Hurons from Lorette, led by their great chief, Thaouvenhosen. The whole army was commanded by Sieur Hertel de Rouville, a French officer of the line.

French as well as Indians were shod with moccasins and snowshoes, and they also brought a supply for any captives they might have the good fortune to secure. They carried provisions ample, as they hoped, for this venturesome trip through the snowy wilderness, both on sleds drawn by dogs, and in packs borne on the back. But the food brought from Canada had been exhausted some time before they reached the end of their long journey. The French soldiers, dependent solely for food on chance game shot by the Indians, were nearly starving and were almost ready mutiny if this attack on Deerfield proved unsuccessful

They left their sleds and dogs near the foot of Wantastiquet Mountain, at the mouth of West River in what is now Brattleboro, Vt. The main body pushed on, reaching Petty's Plain in what is now Greenfield on the night of February 28th. They halted at the foot of Shelburne mountain, behind a bluff overlooking Deerfield's north meadow. They left their packs and all unnecessary incumbrances here, and the Indians of the company smeared themselves with war-paint and joyfully prepared for battle.

Little did the Deerfield settlers dream, on this seemingly peaceful day of February 28th, that only a mile and a half away to the northwest lay this army of French and Indians, only waiting for the darkness of night to descend upon them!

In the early darkness the invaders crept down the hill, crossed the Pocumtuck on the ice, and concealed them- I selves in the woods of Pine Hill, which rose abruptly from the north meadow, a mile above the fort.

Hertel held back as best he could his Indian allies, eager for the onset, and sent scouts down to spy out the land. These scouts, creeping about the palisades, and peeping stealthily over, returned to say that a guard was pacing up and down the street inside. After a time, the scouts were again sent to reconnoitre. This time they found all quiet in the deserted street, lying gray and still in the dim light of the early dawn. They also reported that the snow was so drifted over the palisades on the north side as to afford easy access to the fort.

Hertel, in good spirits, felt that everything pointed towards success. He was about to let loose his impatient army and give the command to march at once when Thaouvenhosen stepped forth and made sign that he would speak to the commander.

Thaouvenhosen was a tall, stately Indian, covered with honorable wounds received in battle, a dignified figure, whose countenance, even when, as now, smeared with warpaint, showed an intelligence above that of his fellows. He said:

"Let my father listen to the council of his Indian braves who have many times taken up the hatchet against our foes, the English. We have been told that this great fort of the English is new and strong, and guarded by a hundred armed men. Englishmen are brave. Their guns have long arms, and reach far. They fight hard. Above all will they fight for their squaws and papooses, even as the she-bear fights for her young. Unless we can come upon them unawares, as the hawk falls from the sky on the meadow mouse, the Great Spirit and the God of the French will not smile on us and give us the victory. We must come on them in deep sleep, and shoot them down like a flock of pigeons on the roost, or our great father, the King of France, will paint his face black, and mourn for his children who return no more to the banks of his great river."

"Ho, ho," grunted all the Indians, in approval of this utterance.

"Most true, good Thaouvenhosen. You speak wise words. But what would you have us do?" asked Hertel, who well knew the necessity of humoring his Indian allies.

"This is Thaouvenhosen's counsel. March not steadily on the English fort, lest our footsteps crunching on the crust waken the foe and put him on his guard. Advance by a rush, then halt; then rush on, and halt again. The sound in the Englishman's sleeping ears will seem but the north wind blowing in gusts. I have spoken."

"Well thought of, Thaouvenhosen," said Hertel, giving the order to advance as the Huron chief had advised. In this stealthy fashion had the approach been made. The snow drifted over the palisades; the sleeping watchman; the fatal sense of security; had all combined to give the foe an easy conquest.

Once safely inside, the enemy broke up into small parties which fell simultaneously upon most of the houses within and north of the fort. One of the first houses assaulted was that of the minister.

Mr. Williams and family were suddenly wakened from deep, sweet sleep by a furious hacking of axes and tomahawks at doors and windows, the smashing sound of yielding planks and cracking glass, while terrific, blood-curdling yells rent the air; the Indian war-whoop screeched from a hundred throats.

"The Indians! O John, the Indians are upon us!" cried his wife, clasping baby Jerusha tightly in her arms, and struggling to rise.

Mr. Williams leaped from his bed, and opening the door into the living-room saw a swarm of painted savages already pouring in through the shattered door.

"Help! Help! The Indians! The Indians!" he shouted, in an effort to arouse the soldiers upstairs. Then he seized his loaded pistol from the bed tester, crying as he did so:

"O God, save us and help us, I beseech Thee!"

Instantly several Indians fell upon him. Cocking his pistol, he thrust it against the breast of the first Indian, but fortunately it missed fire, as otherwise he might have been instantly slain. Three Indians seized him at once, whooping, and crying triumphantly:

"We will carry you to Quebec."

Binding him, they left him standing without clothing just as he had leaped from bed. The baby was torn from its mother's arms by a fierce-looking savage, and the mother was also bound. Thus they stood for an hour in the cold. But little did the Williamses know whether they were cold or warm, in the midst of the terrible scenes going on all around them, and in their overpowering anxiety for their children.

Parthena and Frank rushed in screaming from the back kitchen. Frank was instantly seized and bound. Little John and Warham, wakened in their trundle-bed by the uproar, seeing their parents stand so strangely bound, fled to their friend Parthena for protection, seizing hold of her nightgown, screaming:

"Don't let them get us, Parthena!" Parthena backed into a corner with the little boys, thrusting them behind her, crying:

"The Indians shall not touch you, darlings, as long as Parthena lives!"

The bloody savage who had carried baby Jerusha out the front door there dashed out her brains. His thirst for blood aroused, he returned and tried to tear the terrified children from Parthena.

Parthena fought him, leaving long marks of her finger nails on his painted face, crying:

"You shall not have them, you bloody red devil!"

The furious savage soon overpowered her, and dragged her and little John to the door to slay them. Warham, but four years old, fell on the floor, and unnoticed in the tumult, managed to crawl and hide behind his mother.

The two soldiers upstairs had leaped from bed at the first alarm, seizing their guns. Then seeing how hopeless was any effort to resist such an overwhelming force, they had jumped from the chamber window, and in the tumult had managed to reach the palisades and scale them, and were now flying, barefooted, over the snow towards the south to give the alarm at Hatfield, the nearest settlement, hoping to bring up reinforcements ere too late.

The Williams children upstairs, Samuel, Stephen, Esther, and Eunice, were hardly wakened when they found themselves in the clutches of

Indians. Struck dumb with terror, too frightened to resist, even had that been possible, they were dragged downstairs to the living-room. There several Indians stood guard over their parents, amusing themselves by swinging their tomahawks over and dangerously near Mr. Williams's head, shouting:

"We will burn all you have. We will carry you and your children away to Quebec."

Mr. Williams, pale and shivering both from cold and irrepressible nervous horror, yet calm with the strength not of earth, said to his trembling family:

"Let us commit our state to God. He only can help," and then he cried in prayer, "O God, we beg Thee to remember mercy in the midst of judgment! Suffer us not to perish by the cruel hand of the adversary. Mercifully restrain the enemies' wrath to prevent their murdering us. And give us grace to glorify Thy name, in life or death."

"The Englishman calls on his God. But the paleface God can do naught against the Indian Manitou," sneered the Indian who had charge of Mr. Williams.

Similar scenes were being enacted all over the north half of the town. Most of the terrified people at the south end, except the family of Nathaniel Brooks, who had been seized at the first onslaught, had taken refuge at Captain Jonathan Wells's fortified house. Hither also fled some of the few persons within the stockade who had the good fortune to escape.

The Indians could not break down the stout door of Ensign John Sheldon's house, built of heavy plank, double thickness. Hacking furiously at it, they managed to cut a hole large enough to admit a musket barrel. Thrusting a gun through, they fired in at random, their first shot killing Mrs. Sheldon senior, who was sitting up in bed. A young boy in the house, flying for life out the back door, left it open, and thus the Indians gained admittance to the house.

Upstairs, young John Sheldon and his bride of two short months leaped from the east chamber window. Hannah's ankle was sprained in the fall. Around the corner rushed a swarm of savages, whooping in exultation at sight of fresh victims.

"Leave me, John!" cried his wife. "I cannot run. Fly to Hatfield and bring up our friends there to our rescue ere too late!"

The Indians seized Hannah, and sent bullets whistling around her husband, but he managed to reach the palisades and scale them. Then he fled across the meadow and over the river to the south. He stopped long enough to tear strips from the blanket he had hurriedly snatched from his bed, his only covering, with them bound his bare feet, and then sped on over the snow, with the swiftness lent by love and despair, to Hatfield.

The Sheldon house and the meeting-house were used by the enemy as temporary depots for captives, though Hertel, fearing a rescue, sent from time to time bands of captives and packs of plunder westward across the river to an appointed rendezvous at the foot of Shelburne mountain, there to await the arrival of his main army.

When the Indians fell upon the Catlin house, a brave but fruitless resistance was at first made, in spite of the overwhelming number of the foe, by Mr. Catlin and his oldest son Jonathan. They were soon shot, and fell, sorely wounded and helpless. Young John Catlin seized his father's gun, his brother's powder-horn, and was making a frantic effort to load and fire, when he was over-powered, seized, and bound a captive.

His mother and sister Ruth were also taken captive. Mrs. Catlin would have stayed with her wounded husband and son, but she, Ruth, and John were driven helplessly, at the point of loaded guns, across the stockade, to the Sheldon house. The Catlin house was then set on fire, and Mr. Catlin and Jonathan, in their helpless condition, perished in the flames.

As Mrs. Catlin was driven along, she saw swarms of Indians in and around the house of her daughter, Mrs. Thomas French, and cried:

"Oh, my poor, sick daughter and her little ones! What will become of them?"

The enemy had taken not only their captives, but also their own wounded into the Sheldon house for shelter both from the bullets flying wildly in every direction and from the trampling of the Indians mad with excitement.

Distracted as she was by her own sorrows, so strong was the helpful instinct in her motherly heart that Mrs. Catlin could not but notice and pity the sufferings of a young French officer, pitifully wounded, who lay on the floor, moaning for water. She picked up a pewter porringer from the mass of wreckage of the once happy home which everywhere strewed the floor, and brought him a drink, trying also in other ways to ease his anguish.

"Mother, how can you? Do you not see he is one of our cruel enemies?" asked Ruth.

"If thine enemy hunger, feed him; if he thirst, give him drink. Poor boy! He is far from home. His mother will mourn for him," said the good woman, wiping away the tears flowing down her cheeks.

Many of the people who had fled for refuge to their cellars, or to those dug in the stockade, were smothered there by the smoke and flames of burning buildings above and around. Thus died the little Nims girls, and their brother Henry, good Widow Smead, and many another. But Benjamin Munn's hillside cellar was so buried in the snow that the enemy did not discover it, and he and his family escaped unharmed.

The sun, just rising above Pocumtuck Mountain, shone down on terrible scenes in Deerfield's usually quiet street. A wild crowd of Frenchmen and Indians thronged it, frantically hastening on their work of destruction, fearing the arrival of English reinforcements from below. The air was full of gunpowder smoke, the sound of shots and screams, the moans of dying animals, the cries of dying victims, seized or shot down here, there and everywhere, while the red glare of blazing homes began to add its horror to the fearful scene.

The battle was raging most fiercely around the house of Benoni Stebbins. This house had been attacked later than most of the others, and the people within were better prepared than the other inhabitants for defense. In this house were gathered Benoni Stebbins, his wife and children; young David Hoyt *(son of the deacon)*, wife and child; Joseph Catlin *(oldest son of John Catlin)*, his wife and child; a soldier named Benjamin Church, and three other men.

They had ample supply of guns, powder, and balls in the house, which was built strongly to resist attack, the walls lined with brick, and the overhanging second story provided with port-holes through which to fire on an enemy below.

"We will fight it out to the last," said Stebbins.

"Yes. Better die fighting than suffer our wives and little ones to fall into their hands," said Hoyt, as he hurriedly reloaded his gun.

"Can we hold out long enough, rescue will come from below," said Catlin.

The force attacking the house, as it still held out, was gradually augmented, until at last two hundred French and Indians were assailing this one house defended by only seven men. But these men did not quail or falter. They kept up an incessant fire, aided by their wives, who loaded guns and handed them as fast as emptied. It was here the young French officer had fallen.

At last, so hot and heavy was the fire poured from the beleaguered house, that the enemy was forced to fall back. Then the Indians rushed up with firebrands, trying to set the house on fire, but were repulsed. Three or four Indians perished in this attempt, among them Wannoowooseet, a noted Huron brave.

Within the house fell Stebbins and another man, killed by a shot through a window, and Joseph Catlin and wife were both wounded. But this only made the others more determined, and they fought more desperately. At last the enemy were glad to shelter themselves in the Sheldon house and the meeting-house, whence, under cover, they continued their fire. Offers were sent to the brave defenders that they should be given quarter would they capitulate, but this they refused, keeping up a steady firing. One man fired forty times, and the others were not far behind him. It was now half-past seven. The furious attack on the beleaguered house begun in the gray of early dawn, had been waged nearly three hours.

The strength of the defenders began to wane and their stout hearts to despair.

"I am almost spent," said Church. "I fear I cannot hold out much longer."

"We must fight," said David Hoyt, great circles of exhaustion around his eyes, his face grimy with powder smoke.

"Look! Look!" cried Joseph Catlin at this instant, from a window where he had ventured to peep out. "The enemy are in great commotion. They are flying! Rescue comes, praise be to God!"

Into the fort's southern gate rushed a band of men from Hadley and Hatfield. The watchmen pacing up and down the streets of these settlements had seen from afar the sky red with the glare of burning Deerfield and given the alarm. Mistrusting the cause of the fire, even before the fugitives from Deerfield had arrived, the men from below had hurriedly mounted their horses and hastened to the rescue marching twelve miles through the deep snow, arriving about eight o'clock.

These rescuers from Hadley and Hatfield led by Captain Jonathan Wells, and joined by five garrison soldiers and some of the Deerfield men south of the stockade, rushed into the fort and fired upon the besiegers of the Stebbins house, who at once began to beat a retreat out the fort's north gate.

The women and children in the Stebbins house fled down to Captain Wells's fort, while Hoyt, Catlin, and the other men inside, in spite of their exhaustion, joined the little party of English in hotly pursuing the enemy out across the meadow to the northwest.

When about a mile from the fort, Captain Wells, whose experience at Turner's Falls made him well know the need of caution, tried to halt his little force and called a retreat, but in vain. The excited men, many of whom had lost friends by death or captivity at Indian hands, paid no heed, and still pressed on.

Perceiving the smallness of this pursuing force, the enemy rallied, and joined by fresh recruits who had been in reserve, fell upon the little band of rescuers. Exhausted as they were by their forced march through the snow, and by the engagement, the English under Captain Wells were still not panic stricken, but retreated in good order to the fort, turning repeatedly to fire upon the enemy. In this retreat they lost eleven men left dead on the meadow, among them being Joseph Catlin, David Hoyt, brave Benjamin Wake of Hatfield, Sergeant Boltwood, the miller of Hadley, and his son.

In Deerfield's ruined settlement were left but about one hundred and thirty of the two hundred and ninety inhabitants who were peacefully dwelling there but a few short hours before. Forty-nine of its inhabitants had been slain, and one hundred and eleven carried off captive. Of its forty-one houses only twenty-four were left standing.

By midnight eighty more men came in from the settlements below. By the light of the still blazing ruins of burning homes, a hurried consultation was held. The first impulse was to follow on and assault the enemy that night, in the hope of rescuing the captives before they were borne too far away.

But the wiser and more experienced said:

"The snow is at least three feet deep, and we have no snow-shoes. We can only follow in their path, and cannot overtake them until morning. They are treble our number, are provided with snow-shoes, and can easily outflank and surround us. Moreover, there is great danger that they will slay outright Mr. Williams and his family and the other captives if we pursue and attack them."

All felt the force of this advice. Dismay and uncertainty filled all hearts. None knew what was best to do in face of so terrible a dilemma.

By two o'clock the day after the assault men from Connecticut began to come in, and parties of them continued to arrive, until by night the force in Deerfield was raised to two hundred and fifty men. But a thaw had come on, and without snow-shoes it was impossible to overtake the enemy, who were sure to be making all possible speed to the north.

The idea of pursuit in hope of rescuing the captives was realized to be a hopeless undertaking and at last was reluctantly abandoned. The bodies of the dead were gathered from the meadow, from up and down the street, from the cellars, from under the blackened timbers of still smouldering houses, and were buried in one great grave in the burying-ground west of the fort.

The women and children left in the settlement *(who can describe their terror and dismay?)* were taken to Northampton, Hadley, and Hatfield, all the wounded being left at Hatfield under the care of Dr. Hastings. The men saved what they could of the cattle, horses, and other property not destroyed by the enemy.

A garrison of about thirty men was left under command of Captain Wells in his fort. The would-be rescuers departed, and Deerfield as a settlement was again temporarily abandoned.

# 7

# THE CAPTIVES

THE terrible scenes described were all occurring simultaneously, and occupied but a little over three hours. But it seemed days rather than hours to the Williams family. Huddled in one corner of their kitchen, under the threatening guns and tomahawks of their Indian masters, they watched the wild troop of savages as, raking open the fire on the hearth,—the cheerful home fire whose coals seemed to glare in surprise at the strange scene in the familiar room, —they lit fire-brands, and swarmed over the house, plundering and destroying the most cherished possessions. From without came the incessant roar of musketry around the beleaguered Stebbins house next door, and the bellowing and bleating of terrified animals which the Indians were shooting down in wanton sport.

"Father," whispered Stephen, with white, trembling lips, "do you think they will kill us too?"

"I know not, my son. Remember we are in God's hands. His will be done."

Little four-year-old Warham, clinging to his mother's night-dress, began to sob violently.

"Hush, hush, my child," said the poor mother, unable, bound as she was, even to lay a soothing hand upon the little one; "if you cry so 't will anger the Indians. Try to stop. You have father and mother still, dear child."

Warham pressed his face tightly against his mother to shut out the dreadful sight of the fierce savages, and by a convulsive effort suppressed his sobs. Esther and Eunice too tried to keep back the tears that would flow in spite of them.

All waited in a sort of paralyzed quiet until their Indian masters ordered them to dress. Mr. Williams was kept bound by one arm with a rope until he had put his clothing on the other side, when the rope was changed to the opposite arm. When dressed, his hands were again bound behind his back, as were those of the boys.

Mrs. Williams was allowed to dress herself and to aid her younger children. The mother instinct, stronger than death itself, prompted her to say:

"Put on all the thickest garments you can lay hold of my daughters, for, if God spare our lives to take it, we have before us a cruel journey."

Even under such circumstances as these she did not for-get to snatch from the table her Bible. Here only was comfort and help to be found under these calamities.

At about half-past seven the Williamses were driven out of their house, past the dead bodies of their little ones and Parthena, seeing the Indians setting fire to their house and barn as they left. Amid the uproar of firing still going on, past the dead bodies of many a familiar friend, past burning homes on all sides, they were driven out the north gate and across the meadow, struggling through the deep snow which came to their knees, a thaw having softened the crust.

Crossing the river on the ice, and struggling up the steep, snowy bank, they were halted at the spot, about a mile above the settlement, where the Indians had left their packs. Here they found gathered a melancholy company of their old neighbors and friends, a hundred or more. Nearly every family in Deerfield was represented there.

Here they saw Mrs. Frary, Thomas French, his wife, and five children *(his baby having already been slain as an useless incumbrance)*, and Mrs. Godfrey Nims, with her four-year-old daughter Abigail, and her son Ebenezer. Happily for her she did not know the sad fate of the children left behind, and of her mother, Widow Smead, all smothered in the cellar of her burning home, but said to Mrs. Frary:

"I thank God for this mercy: at all events my other children are safe in Deerfield, and will have their father to care for them."

Here too were John Stebbins, his wife and entire family of children, Deacon Hoyt, his wife and five children, Me-human Hinsdale and wife, Mrs. Belding, John and Ruth Catlin, and many another familiar friend.

Mrs. Catlin, on account of her kindness to the young French officer, it was supposed *(he was said to be a brother of Hertel de Rouville)* had at the last moment been released from captivity and left behind in ruined Deerfield. This late respite was of little avail, for the poor woman's heart was broken. She had seen her husband and son Jonathan killed, her home burned, her baby grandchild deliberately butchered, her two married daughters, Mrs. French and Mrs. Corse, her son John and daughter Ruth, and six grandchildren, all dragged away into savage captivity. Her son Joseph was slain in the meadow fight. She was left alone, stripped in one short hour of all dear to her. What wonder that, prostrated by the terrible blow, she died but a few weeks later?

The poor captives huddled in forlorn groups on the snow-covered hilltop. In the early morning sunlight which streamed down on the smoke and flames pouring up into the sky from their burning homes, they gazed sorrowfully on their minister and family as they saw them too joining their number.

"Poor Mrs. Williams!" whispered Mrs. Frary to Mrs. Belding. "It will fare worse with her and Mrs. French than with the rest of us even. For they are not strong yet, and the arms of both are empty. I fear the savages have slain their babes."

"Doubtless," said Mrs. Belding, who well knew whereof she spoke. "They are capable of any cruelty. O my God—" she faltered, and then checked herself.

For like all the captives, she realized the danger of making any moans. To be quiet, to restrain tears or any manifestations of grief was their only safety. They gazed on one another in mute, sorrowful silence. Mr. Williams, bound as he was, and great as were his own troubles, yet tried to speak a few sustaining words to his people nearest him; broken words of trust.

Soon the captives were excited by seeing the little rescue party of English come out on the north meadow in pursuit of the enemy. Well they knew how hopeless must be this brave attempt against such overwhelming numbers. Indeed, they breathed easier when they saw their friends retreating towards the fort, for the Indians had said:

"If the English follow us and try to rescue you, we will slay you all."

The captives were forced to exchange their own shoes for Indian moccasins, and to put on snow-shoes.

Stephen Williams whispered to his brother Samuel:

"I don't see, Sam, how I can walk at all in these awkward things. The Indians will soon slay me, for I can never keep up."

"You will soon get used to them, and then they will be a great help," said Samuel. "Try to keep up good courage, Stephen. I will walk with you and help you on, if our Indian masters permit it."

The company of almost four hundred persons, French, Indians, and captives, now set off north across Petty's Plain, making for the regular Indian footpath to the north which ran along the foot of Shelburne mountain. The men and older boys among the captives were forced to carry on their backs large packs of the plunder taken at Deerfield, as did many of the Indians. The Indians also bore on their shoulders several of their own wounded. To the surprise of the captives, they carried the younger children whom they knew unable to make such a journey as lay before them.

Stephen whispered to Samuel, as they walked side by side:

"Do see, Sam, poor little Warham, on that fierce-looking Indian's back! See how sorrowfully he looks towards our father. Yet he dare not cry out."

"Poor boy! I would rather walk than ride on such a horse," said Samuel, "and so would poor Warham, could he have his choice."

Mr. Williams's hands had been unbound, that he might walk more easily. He having been captured by two Indians, both claimed him as their property. Oioteet, who seemed the more savage of these two masters, now had Mr. Williams in charge, and would not allow his prisoner to speak to the other captives. Mr. Williams's heart was rent, as he saw his feeble wife dragging herself along, urged on by her master. Yet he was unable to render her any aid, or even speak to her.

Esther, Eunice, Thankful Stebbins, Ruth Catlin, and others of the girls toiled on together. The Shelburne mountains, dark and shaggy to the top with primeval forest, seemed to look coldly down on the long file of travellers straggling along at their base, black against the white snow. Far off to the north the girls, searching the horizon around, as if for possible help or rescue, saw rising other wild mountain ranges wooded to the summit.

"Look, Ruth," whispered Sarah Hoyt. "See those mountains to the north. How desperate is our case if we must travel over them!"

"I know one thing. I will drop dead in my tracks before I will please the savages by complaining," said high-spirited Ruth, with an angry toss of her head. Her intense hatred of the Indians made her forget to pity herself, and almost buoyed her up as she walked along.

Ebenezer Nims looked back towards Sarah. Gladly would he have aided her, but the Indians guarded the men jealously, keeping them apart from the other captives, and well in advance.

The company travelled on for about six miles. The enemy, knowing the possibility of pursuit, were anxious to get on as fast and far as possible. Yet, being themselves considerably exhausted, and cumbered with their own wounded who needed rest and attention, they made an early halt. The halt was made at a favorable camping spot such as they always secured if possible,—a wooded knoll, near a fine brook, backed by a swamp, a spot not only suited for camping, but adapted to easy defense in case of attack.

Here they fell to work, making their camp with the deftness born of long practice. They dug away the snow, making the men among the captives help them. Cutting poles from the trees around, they erected wigwam frames, which they covered not only with the mats and skins they carried, but also with strips of bark, and spruce and pine boughs laid thickly on the outside for greater warmth. In the centre of each wigwam a camp-fire was built.

The Indians now began eagerly undoing the packs of provisions brought from Deerfield. Oioteet brought Mr. Williams food, commanding:

"Eat now, while food is plenty, to be strong to travel tomorrow!"

Although neither Mr. Williams nor any of the captives had tasted a morsel that day, they had no appetite in their forlorn condition, and could force down but little food.

"There is such a great lump in my throat I cannot swallow," whispered Ben Hoyt, a boy of but eight, to Stephen, his eyes full of tears ready to fall.

"'Tis so with me too," said Stephen. "But we must not cry, Ben. It will only anger the savages, and make them kill us, as they did my little brother John. Look at your sister Ruth, how bravely she bears herself. And even my little sister Eunice is not crying, though at home she was wont to cry and run to mother did she but pinch her finger. We must be as brave as the girls."

But if the captives could eat little, the Indians, who had so long been semi-starved, quite made up for past deficiencies, gorging themselves as was their wont when food was plentiful.

"See that painted red savage," whispered Mrs. Stebbins to Mrs. Belding. "He is cramming down that loaf-cake almost at a mouthful. I know it is mine, that I made but yesterday,—what ages ago it seems,—thinking to ask our pastor to tea tonight. Little did I think with what company we should sup this night! It may be wicked, but I can't help wishing that cake might choke him!"

"No wonder you feel so," said Mrs. Belding. "Do you see, he has on the great-coat of Samson Frary? Doubtless that good man was slain. Mrs. Frary does not know what became of her husband in the onslaught. It is to be hoped she will not notice that coat."

Small branches of evergreen trees had been cut and thrown down around the fires in each wigwam. At early dusk the captives were ordered to lie down on these rude beds. They were carefully scattered about among their captors. Mr. Williams and the other men and large boys were bound fast, hand and foot, and tied to stakes, lest possibly they escape in the night.

The inmates of the wigwams were obliged to lie in a crooked posture, as their heads were against the outer edge of the rude wigwam, and they could not extend their feet without thrusting them into the fire.

Lying in this cramped position, crowded in between two big Indians, Stephen Williams, like most of the other captives, was long in falling asleep. The boy lay, not venturing to stir, his eyes unnaturally bright and wide open, watching the flickering firelight on the wigwam's side, listening to the heavy breathing of his Indian bedfellows, and to the wild sounds from without; for some of the Indians had found good liquors in the Deerfield houses, and were now holding a drunken orgy. Hertel de Rouville dared riot cross his Indian allies in their enjoyment of the spoils of victory, and was obliged to allow them largely their own way.

As Stephen listened to the wild yells, drunken shouts, and chanted songs coming from around the chief campfire where the feast was going on, suddenly in the firelight he saw two Indians enter the wigwam. They seized Frank, his father's faithful slave, who, poor fellow, worn out with sorrow and fatigue, had fallen into a heavy sleep, bound as he was. They dragged him away, half awake.

Stephen trembling with fear, not knowing whose turn might come next, heard the despairing cries of "Help! Help!" from poor Frank soon stifled in the merriment outside, which grew louder and wilder.

"I must pray to God," thought Stephen, trained from earliest infancy to believe that God was always near, always saw, always cared. He said the Lord's prayer, and then besought God to care for and protect through the night his parents, his brothers and sisters, and himself. The thought of the All-seeing Friend comforted and soothed the little boy somewhat, and at last, worn out by the terrible excitement and weariness of that long dreadful day, he fell asleep.

All through the night the woods around the camp resounded with the hoots of owls, the howl of wolf, or growl of bear; for the Indians on guard around the camp were thus signaling each other.

# 8

# ON TO THE NORTH

THOSE of the captives who had fallen into an uneasy sleep towards morning were soon awakened by a great commotion in the camp.

Stephen Williams sat up, rubbing his eyes, waking from a dream of some happenings in Master Richards' school, wherein he was under discipline. He gazed about on his strange surroundings in bewilderment. Where was he? Was this also a dream? In another moment he realized the sad truth, and his heart sank down within him.

"What is the matter? What has happened?" he asked of Ebenezer Nims, who had just been thrust into the wigwam by his Indian master, his hands bound behind his back.

"From what I overheard, I suppose one of us escaped in the night," said Ebenezer. "I guess it must be John Bridgman, one of the garrison soldiers that was stationed at Thomas French's house. I chanced to walk near him yesterday, and he whispered to me, 'Mark my word, Eben. I'll break loose tonight from these savages and get off somehow, even if the attempt cost me my life. I'll never be taken to Canada alive.' Bridgman is an old campaigner, and doubtless knew well how to loosen their knots."

It was indeed true that Bridgman had somehow contrived to undo the ropes fastening him, and to elude the Indian guards, making good his escape in the darkness.

Mr. Williams, as the leading man among the captives, was now summoned to the presence of the commander, Hertel de Rouville, and haughtily ordered:

"Tell your people that if any more escape, I shall no longer restrain my Indian allies. They will burn the rest of the prisoners. Let them take heed."

Mr. Williams gave his people this message. But they hardly needed it, for the angry faces of the Indians, their threatening manner, and such words as the captives understood, told them but too plainly what was likely to be the fate of those left behind should any more of their number escape.

This day of March 1st was of vital importance to the French and Indians. For today, still within a few miles of Deerfield, the danger of pursuit was most imminent. Large reinforcements might already have reached Deerfield from the older settlements below. An early start was made. All was bustle and commotion. Coverings were torn from wigwams, packs tied up and bound on backs, and the captives were scattered along among the enemy, the men, especially, being kept well to the front.

Leaving the great logs of their campfires still smouldering and the wigwam poles standing, again the dreary march was taken up for the north, every step bearing the unhappy captives farther and farther from home and the chance of rescue, nearer and nearer to they knew not what terrible fate. Mr. Williams, like the other men, was compelled to bear a heavy pack on his back. Thus laden, and unaccustomed to snow-shoes, difficult, indeed, was it to travel.

The Indians were easily able to carry burdens of one or even two hundred pounds on their shoulders by aid of a tumpline or carrying strap. This was a long leathern thong, broader in the part which crossed the forehead. The weight was really suspended from their heads. But to the captives, unused to this way of burden bearing, even small packs were a great added hardship.

Oioteet, as one of the fiercest of the Indian warriors, was placed with Thaouvenhosen in command of the braves guarding the rear of the retreating column, the point of danger from pursuers. Mr. Williams was therefore left in charge of his other master, Suckkeecoo, whose face, less savage than that of Oioteet, seemed to indicate a milder nature.

Looking back, Mr. Williams saw his sick wife, evidently walking with greatest difficulty. By signs and broken words, he pleaded with Suckkeecoo to be allowed to aid her.

"The English father may go help his squaw," said Suckkeecoo.

Mr. Williams, thankful for this mercy, hastened back to his wife's side, and walked with her for some distance along the path at the foot of Shelburne mountain. Her pale face wore a spiritual aspect, and her great eyes had a far-away look, as of one who already sees beyond the boundary of earthly vision, who steps within the border-land beyond the grave.

"Dear wife," said Mr. Williams, tenderly supporting her, "lean all your weight on me. I will sustain you. I trust, dear Eunice, that God sustains your soul under these calamities, even as I support your fainting body."

"Yes, dear husband, it is even so. My soul clings to God and I can still praise Him, even in these sore troubles. He knoweth best."

"Think, my wife, of the happiness of those who have a right to a house not made with hands, eternal in the heavens, and who know that God is their father and friend. Is it not our reasonable duty to submit to His will, e'en though He slay us?"

"I truly feel it so, dear husband. I can say with my last breath, 'The will of the Lord be done.' My strength of body begins to fail. You must expect soon to part with me."

Mr. Williams held her closer, unable at the moment to control his grief enough for speech. Yet he was pastor as well as husband. He must help strengthen and support this soul, perhaps soon to depart on its journey into the unseen. In broken words, he managed to murmur:

"Think much, my wife, on the blessed words of David, 'Though I walk through the valley of the shadow of death, I will fear no evil: for Thou art with me; Thy rod and Thy staff they comfort me.'"

"I hope God may preserve your life, and that of some if not all of our dear children," faltered the wife in feeble tones. "I leave my children to your care, John, under God. I know you will rear them, if they and you are spared, to be God-fearing people. I would I could say good-by to the children. But perhaps it is best. It would be hard for them. Be very tender of poor little Warham, John. Soon I shall be with my little ones gone before. Their sweet faces will smile again into mine. Perhaps they miss and need their mother, even amid the heavenly host."

The company had now reached the point where the Indian foot-path, following the trend of the mountains, turned eastward toward the banks of a small river, rapid and swollen with melting snow. Here a halt was made.

Oioteet now came up and spoke angrily to Suckkeecoo, evidently displeased because Mr. Williams had been permitted to go back and walk with his wife. He seized Mr. Williams roughly and dragged him to the front, compelling him to march with the foremost. Oioteet well knew that the minister of Deerfield was a captive of more than ordinary value, likely to bring a large ransom, and feared his escape.

As he was dragged away, Mr. Williams had only time to say:

"Farewell, dear wife, desire of my eyes. God be ever with thee."

Left alone among her cruel captors, Mrs. Williams opened her Bible, and, as she tottered feebly on, snatched from its pages passages that have sustained and uplifted suffering souls in all generations. As her eyes fell on the words in Luke, "Father, forgive them, for they know not what they do," "Father, into Thy hands I commend my spirit," the thought of her Saviour's sufferings strengthened her to bear her own.

Samuel, Esther, Stephen, Eunice, all passed by their mother, for she began to lag sadly, unable to keep up with the main body. The children were too far away to speak, even had they been permitted. But they never forgot the saintly radiance illuminating their mother's face in this their last glimpse of it, or the tender smile of undying mother love she gave each child as they passed.

The river, whose banks the company had now reached, had a rapid current. Its edges were bordered with thin ice, but out in the centre the green water swept swiftly down. Into this cold, swift stream the captives were now compelled to plunge and struggle across as best they could.

The younger children were borne over by the Indians. Stephen, although ten years old, was small and slight for his age. But his Indian master, Mummumcott, seized him by the hand and pulled him along, holding him up when the swift current swept his feet from under him. The girls were aided in like fashion. Then wet, dripping, shivering in the chilly wind, they were forced to walk on, the path leading directly up a steep hill or mountain side.

Mr. Williams found the water above his knees, and the current very swift. He was filled with anxiety for his feeble wife, and prayed Oioteet to let him go back and aid her. But Oioteet refused and drove his captive, his pack on his back, up the steep mountain side. Then, seeing that Mr. Williams's strength was nearly spent, at the top of the ascent Oioteet unbound the pack from his captive's shoulders, and suffered him to sit down and rest.

Great as was this relief to his weary body, Mr. Williams hardly thought of it, so heavy was his heart, so rent with anxiety for his wife, and with pity for his tender children forced to endure such hardships. He saw too the people of his flock toiling slowly and painfully, laden with their burdens, up this steep ascent in the soft snow, for the weather had grown warmer, and this hillside lay to the south. Again he begged his stern master to let him go back and help his wife. But Oioteet, waving his hatchet suggestively near Mr. Williams's head, said:

"The English priest shall not stir from Oioteet. He must stay where he is, or Oioteet will soon put an end to his foolish clamor. Let the pale-face squaw care for herself, same as Indian squaw."

As one after another of the captives passed by the spot where Mr. Williams sat, he asked anxiously for news of his wife, if any could tell him how she fared. At last came Deacon Hoyt. Man though he was, tears were rolling down his cheeks. His Indian master, angry at such weakness, was driving him on. Yet, daring his wrath, as he passed by, Deacon Hoyt tarried long enough to say hastily:

"Mr. Williams, 't is all over with thy poor wife. Struggling through the river she fell and was nearly drowned. Seeing her unable to ascend this mountain, at its foot her cruel master slew her with one stroke of his hatchet."

Mr. Williams burst into tears. For the time, his agony seemed unbearable. That his beloved wife, whom he had cherished so tenderly, whom he would gladly have shielded lest even a rough breath of wind blow on her too rudely, should be slain thus remorselessly while alone among her enemies, her body left a prey to wild beasts!

Oioteet gazed on his grief with infinite disgust and contempt.

"The English are no better than squaws," he said. "Even an Indian papoose would be ashamed to weep like the pale-face father." And binding on Mr. Williams's pack again, he drove him along.

Mr. Williams's only comfort now was the memory of the strong, unquestioning faith in God shown by his wife in their last interview. As he toiled on over the snow, his heart cried out pitifully to God for help.

"O God, I pray Thee, suffer not my faith to fail me in this hour of sore need. She is at rest, released from her sufferings and fears. She is with Thee, with her Saviour, with her precious little ones. O Lord, Thou knowest I believe. Help Thou mine unbelief! My faith staggers under this weight of anguish. Strengthen me, I pray Thee, for the sake of my poor children, and of all these afflicted ones, who look to me as their guide and helper."

Another prayer constantly going up from his heart as he journeyed on was:

"O God, in Thy Providence so overrule events, I beseech Thee, that the body of one so dear to me, one of Thy saints, whose glorified spirit Thou hast taken to Thy nearer presence, may not be left in the wilderness as meat for the fowls of the air and beasts of the field. Grant her dear body a Christian burial, I pray Thee."

Not till long after did he know *(and great was then his relief)* that this prayer was granted. A party from Deerfield, following on the track of the captives to the north the next day, found the body of their beloved minister's wife, and bore it back on horse-back to Deerfield, there laying it to rest in the burying-ground.

During this day, Mrs. Carter's infant was killed, and later a girl of eleven. If any failed, or became in the slightest degree a hindrance on the retreat, the Indians hesitated not a moment to rid themselves of the incumbrance. The knowledge of this fact stimulated each weary, foot-sore, heavy-laden and heavy-hearted captive, even to the young girls and boys, to struggle on, keeping up the best appearance possible. For the instinct which impels us to cling to life is deep and undying, even amidst distress which would seem to make death a welcome release.

The army journeyed about nine miles beyond the Picommegan River, and then camped again for the night in the wilderness in what is now Bernardston. As Oioteet was obliged to oversee the making of the camp, Mr. Williams, to his relief, was placed in charge of his other master Suckkeecoo.

As soon as Oioteet was at a safe distance, Mr. Williams begged:

"Good Suckkeecoo, suffer me to talk with my children that I may help them and make their hearts strong."

Again Suckkeecoo was gracious, and for a short time Mr. Williams and his children had the comfort of being together. Gathering little Warham up in his arms, and pressing him to his bosom, and drawing the child Eunice tenderly to him, Mr. Williams hurriedly tried to give his sorrowful children some words of comfort. For they had all heard of their mother's cruel death, the news of the slaying of Mrs. Williams having circulated quickly among the captives.

"My children," said Mr. Williams, "we must strive to feel that your loved mother was taken away by God in His great loving-kindness to her, to save her not only from the evils we now endure, but perchance from far greater yet in store for us."

"I thought of that," said Esther. "She is happier than we, perhaps."

"One moment," said Mr. Williams, his sad face transfigured with the shining of Christian faith, "one moment was the faintness unto death, the instant's pain of the cruel hatchet's stroke, perhaps hardly felt. The next, and she was joined to the assembly of the spirits of the just made perfect, to rest in peace, in joy unspeakable and full of glory. 'Eye hath not seen, nor ear heard, nor hath it entered into the heart of man to understand the things God hath prepared for them that love Him.' And your mother loved God, and trusted Him, even to the last. Almost with her dying breath she assured me of her unfaltering faith."

"It is well with our mother," said Esther, in pitiful tone, "but it is grievous for us. What can we do without her?"

And, in spite of her efforts to control her grief, Esther began to sob. Samuel and Stephen too were overcome with sorrow. Eunice and Warham were fortunately too young to realize the meaning of death.

"We cannot understand," said Mr. Williams. "We must try to trust. It is God's good pleasure thus to try us. I doubt not the spirit of your sainted mother will oft be near you to help you, though unseen. Let the thought of her unfaltering trust strengthen your faith, my children, no matter what trials come. Cling closely to God, the God of your fathers."

Here a commotion arose among the Indians. Some of them looked enraged, and a bitter quarrel was evidently going on about something, the captives knew not what. But all were alarmed, for in their helpless state any change might forebode greater horrors. Each Indian hastened to gather the captives he claimed as his own property, and Mr. Williams and his children were rudely separated, seized and dragged away in different directions. But their father's words had sunk deep down into his children's hearts, a comfort and help in their troubles.

# 9

# DIVIDING THE CAPTIVES

A QUARREL had arisen among the Indians about the possession of captives. Some held five or six. Some had none. Captives were considered by Indians as one of the regular assets of war. They were useful as domestic drudges, and if redeemed often brought a handsome ransom. Above all, they were a symbol of triumph, second only to scalps. The brave bringing home from the warpath a string of white captives and a sheaf of scalps sat in high places at the council fires.

The quarrel had been hot and furious, and Thaouvenhosen and the other chiefs saw that to avoid serious trouble a more equable division of captives must be made. This had accordingly been arranged for the following morning.

When Mummumcott had dragged Stephen away to his own wigwam, a new trouble awaited the little boy. Now that the greater distance from Deerfield gave more sense of security, Mummumcott felt at ease to search his little captive for possible valuables. Stephen wore silver knee-buckles, and silver buttons in his shirt. Few boys in those days owned such treasures. These had been given Stephen by his Grandmother Mather of Northampton, who had also given his mother the silver cup now in the pack borne by her slayer. The trinkets were very precious to the child.

"Ugh," grunted Mummumcott with satisfaction, as he tore off the shining buckles and buttons, and dropped them into the long pouch worn at his belt. This pouch was made of an otter's skin, the head and paws hanging down, elaborately embroidered with beads and quills.

Stephen's face flushed, and tears filled his eyes, but he dared not resist. And soon his mind was painfully diverted from this lesser grief by a talk he overheard between Oioteet and another fierce-looking savage, who said:

"Better burn the white father. He will talk to the captives and make them rebel against their masters. The white father has no strength. His heart is all same as squaw's heart. He will never reach Canada. Better have pleasure torturing him tonight than try to take him on. Indians want a burning."

Oioteet gave a grunt, which might mean either assent or refusal, and Stephen, pale and wretched, watched eagerly to see what was to be his father's fate.

Mr. Williams had heard the savage's proposal. He could tell nothing of Oioteet's intentions by his unmoved face. He lifted up his heart in silent prayer, imploring God's grace and mercy in such a time of need. Then he said to Oioteet:

"If you intend to kill me, I desire to know it. But remember, if you slay me, after promising me quarter, as you did, you will bring down guilt of blood on your head."

This argument did not appeal to Oioteet, but, as he had not the slightest idea of killing a captive likely to be of such value for ransom, could he but get him to Canada alive, he had the grace to relieve Mr. Williams's apprehensions by saying gruffly:

"Oioteet no kill the English father to-night."

Stephen saw by the relieved expression of his father's face that the dread danger was past, at least for the present, and breathed easier himself.

The unaccustomed use of snow-shoes all day had been most trying to the captives. Hard at first, it grew harder as the day went on. If one fell, as often happened in trying to cross a log or stump, it was impossible for him to rise until pulled up by others. Now many of the captives were suffering intense pain, the cords of their legs being knotted in painful bunches. Yet so utterly exhausted were all, that in spite of this pain the captives slept hard that night on their beds of boughs.

A spring rain had set in, driving against the wigwam's side and pattering down through the smoke holes making the wigwams blue with smoke. Most of the captives had to lie with their faces on the ground near the wigwam's sloping outer edge in order to breathe. The rain would make hard travelling tomorrow. Yet the captives slept, so worn were they.

Early the next morning the captives were all gathered in one body outside the largest wigwam. Inside were assembled the sachems of the Indians, to settle this important matter of dividing the spoils of war.

Before allowing Mr. Williams to leave them, Oioteet and Suckkeecoo thriftily stripped him of all the best of his clothing, giving him instead an Indian shirt and leggings of deerskin, and an Indian blanket. The Indians knew they could get good money or perhaps the much coveted fire-water in Canada from the French in exchange for this clothing.

As the minister, clad thus strangely, approached the central wigwam, he saw Thomas French and John Stebbins, painfully limping, also drawing near. Difficult as it evidently was for them to walk, yet their faces wore an expression which indicated to their minister's eye mental anxiety greater than their bodily distress.

They made a sign for Mr. Williams to tarry, and, as they overtook him, Stebbins said in low, cautious tone:

"We are satisfied that the savages mean to burn some of us this morning. They have peeled the bark from several trees, and are acting strangely, in a manner that bodes no good to us unhappy captives."

"'Tis doubtless for this reason that we are now summoned together, that they may select the victims," said French.

Mr. Williams, remembering his own escape *(as he felt it)* of the previous night, could but share these misgivings. Yet he tried to quiet the fears of his old parishioners by words of trust.

"They can act nothing against us but as they are permitted of God. He holds us in the hollow of His hand. I am persuaded He will not suffer such severities."

The captives were all greatly relieved when they found it was only for this matter of division they had been gathered. The division was made, not without leaving sore hearts among those Indians who had claimed six captives as their own and were now reduced to two. Many of the captives changed masters, but Mr. Williams was still left with the two who had taken him from his home, and Mummumcott was allowed to retain Stephen. Stephen told his brother Samuel, when he had a chance to speak to him:

"I am glad to stay with Mummumcott, anyway. He is bad enough, but a new master might be more cruel. He does not wave his hatchet over my head continually and threaten to kill me every time I lag a bit, as poor Eben Hoyt's master does. He cut Eben's forehead a little, yesterday. It bled, but Eben dared not cry."

The walking in the snow, softened as it was by the rain, was most difficult, even for the Indians. As for the captives, their sore muscles made walking an exquisite torture. The only remedy for this snow-shoe lameness was again to walk until it passed away. Not knowing this the captives set off with gloomy forebodings, not lessened by the slaughter during the day of Esther Pomroy, a young matron of twenty-seven, whose delicate condition caused her strength to fail.

Progress under the circumstances was very slow. Not until the next day, Friday, March 3rd, did they reach the banks of "the great river," as the settlers were wont to call the noble stream named by the Indians the Quinneticot, meaning "the long river." The point they reached was in what is now Vernon, Vt.

The ice was still strong, but was covered with water ankle deep. Yet on its surface the captives were now forced to continue their journey, wading in the cold water for hours. No wonder that the women in the company were conscious of growing weaker, and murmured faintly to one another, with white, drawn lips:

"We shall soon go to join Mrs. Williams and Esther Pomroy."

Mr. Williams's children, and his people, too, noticed with alarm, as the day went on, that he grew very lame. Travelling in the icy water for hours, as he was forced to do, brought on a severe lameness in the ankle he had sprained the previous autumn. All believed him to be doomed, as they saw him growing lamer, fearing that soon his strength would wholly give out. Then he would certainly be slain.

He himself believed his end to be near. But as he limped painfully on, he made no complaint. His face wore the serene peace of one whose heart is at rest in God. Inwardly he prayed:

"O God, my only refuge, if it be Thy will, graciously re-move my lameness, and preserve me, for the sake of my poor children and my afflicted people. But, if Thou callest me now to glorify Thee by my death, I pray Thee be with me in the great change, and sustain me.

And wilt Thou care for my children, left alone amid the savages, and my dear flock, and strengthen and preserve them."

Strangely enough, soon after this prayer the lameness disappeared, and Mr. Williams was able to travel again as well as ever, to the joy of all. They saw in this deliverance a miracle wrought by God to save their minister. He himself could not be blamed for believing his recovery a direct answer to prayer. With his heart singing praises to his merciful God, he walked on with fresh courage.

As the day wore on, the Indians pressed forward more rapidly. After a while, they began to give the scalp halloo, a long yell for every scalp or prisoner they had taken, followed by quick, shrill cries of joy and triumph which echoed wildly back from the frowning mountain side rising steeply east of the river.

"What means this hideous outcry, do you suppose?" asked John Catlin of Jonathan Hoyt.

"I have not the faintest idea," answered Jonathan, "only we may be sure it bodes no good to us."

"True enough, little is the good we can expect," said John.

He was not strong, and had never slept from under the home roof even one night when carried off into captivity. No wonder that, young though he was, his strength often seemed about to fail.

Now from the north the captives heard answering yells and whoops, accompanied by the loud barking of dogs and a rapid firing of guns.

Soon they saw above them, at the mouth of a small stream which here entered the Connecticut, the pointed tops of wigwams rising against a rocky background. A band of strange Indians came running to meet their comrades, waving hatchets, firing guns, and shouting for joy, as they perceived the army returning rich with a hundred white captives and heavily laden with packs of spoils.

These new Indians were the guard which had been left behind with the dogs and sledges, a short week ago, when the main body had pushed on for Deerfield. The rock at the mouth of the river had been rudely carved by them with pictographs such as the Indians were in the habit of cutting to record their important undertakings.

At the base of the rock, the wild herd of dogs, gaunt and wolfish, their coarse, gray hair standing erect around their necks, leaped frantically, adding to the noisy welcome their loud yelping.

It was a jubilant time for the Indians, but not for the wretched captives, for as each sad day widened the distance between them and home, and the scenes around grew wilder, they realized with sinking hearts that all prospect of rescue grew more hopeless.

All the savages held a grand feast of rejoicing that night, for the Indians who had been left behind not unjustly clamored for their share of the joys and spoils of war. To the meat of bear and deer which the guard were able to contribute was added what remained of the stores taken in Deerfield.

The captives lay around the wigwam fires, thankful to be at last able to stop the endless walking on and on and on of the long, dreary day, yet few of them were able to sleep amid the wild shouts, the monotonous singsong of the war-songs, chanted to an accompaniment of gourd rattles and the tum-tum of the skin drums coming from the orgy without.

Suddenly some of the captives were startled by seeing two Indians holding a fire-brand enter their wigwam as if in search of some one. When they came to Thomas French, giving a grunt of satisfaction, they seized him and dragged him away. His friends lay in shuddering terror, fearing the worst for French and themselves from the savages excited by their orgy.

At the feast a clamor had arisen among some of the Hurons, because the death of their chief, Wannoowooseet, slain in battle in the attempt to take the Stebbins house, had not been suitably avenged. The friends of Wannoowooseet were loudly supported in their claims for satisfaction by the Indians left behind in camp, who thirsted for their share of the pleasures of war.

A young brave, Masseamet, a nephew of Wannoowooseet, made a stirring speech:

"The blood of Wannoowooseet, our kinsman, has been spilled like water by the English. It cries aloud for vengeance. The spirits of the slain can only be satisfied by spilling the blood of the enemy. Shall Wannoowooseet, who made the whole earth tremble before him when he took up the hatchet and went forth on the warpath, who shot down the English like tame pigeons, die like a squaw or a dog, unavenged?"

Loud, approving cries of "Ho, Ho, Ho!" rose from many of Masseamet's hearers. But the older men among the Hurons looked grave and were silent. Their rude natures had been partly tamed by the devoted labors of Father Davagour and Father Descouvert, who had charge of the Jesuit mission at Lorette, three leagues from Quebec, where the remnant of the Huron tribe were now dwelling. They were at least partly civilized, and the good fathers had used all their efforts to tame the natural savage propensities. Above all, they had labored against the Indian custom of burning or torturing captives. It had been easier to influence the older Indians than the younger, fiercer braves.

Encouraged by the applause, Masseamet continued:

"Masseamet, the nephew of Wannoowooseet, demands that one of the leaders among the captives be given us to torture and burn. This is a just reward for our victory. Then will the spirit of our uncle go satisfied to the happy hunting-grounds, and the sore place in the hearts of his family will be made whole."

At this point two Indians, fired by the eloquence of Masseamet, had rushed off and seized Thomas French, the town clerk of Deerfield, as the destined victim, while others began peeling bark from trees, preparing to burn him when he should have been sufficiently tortured.

A wild, fierce joy lit the faces of the younger braves, as Thomas French was brought into their midst. As for French himself, he knew that a cruel death was near. Yet he maintained a calm outward aspect, knowing how worse than useless would be any laments or appeals.

Now rose the stately form of Thaouvenhosen. All were silent, and strict attention was given him, for Thaouvenhosen was one of the foremost among the Huron chiefs. No one bore more scars of wounds received in battle than he. All knew that wherever he fought, the enemy were routed, and all knew how great had been his part in the taking of Deerfield.

"My brothers and my children," he said, "Thaouvenhosen asks for the life of this captive. We are Christians, citizens of Lorette, children of the good fathers, who have often told us that to torture is not fit for Christians. Before the Hurons left Lorette, they prayed at the holy shrine for victory. God, the Blessed Virgin, the holy saints, have smiled upon us and have granted our prayer. Shall we now anger them and lose their favor by this action, so displeasing to them? Let the captive be spared. This is the word of Thaouvenhosen."

Thaouvenhosen sat down. The Indians plainly wavered. They were reluctant to give up their pleasure, yet the words of Thaouvenhosen carried much weight. But now rose Masseamet, emboldened by the success of his former speech, and by the knowledge that he had the secret sympathy of many among his hearers.

"Our great uncle, Thaouvenhosen, has spoken. Now listen to the words of Masseamet. My brothers well know if the Indians are weak-hearted, and show mercy even to one captive, the English will grow bold, and will come and destroy us all. The Indians must make the English fear them, as the sucking lamb fears the hungry wolf. I, Masseamet, the nephew of Wannoowooseet, demand the captive's blood, to cover up and wash away the blood of Wannoowooseet, and to heal the wound in the hearts of his family."

Masseamet sat down, well pleased with his own eloquence. The Indians who held French began to strip him, feeling that Masseamet had carried the day. But now again rose Thaouvenhosen, his eyes flashing, his head, adorned with the eagle feathers of a great chief, held proudly aloft, his tall form seeming to tower up higher, as he said in the loud, bold tone of one who fears nothing:

"Thaouvenhosen is also a relation of Wannoowooseet. To Thaouvenhosen does the captive belong. Thaouvenhosen claims him as his own. If any dare to lay hands on him, to Thaouvenhosen will he answer. Fear not that the blood of my relation will go unavenged. In honorable battle Thaouvenhosen will wipe out the stain of Wannoowooseet's blood, and many English scalps shall cover his wounds and dry the tears of his squaw and friends."

None dared to molest French after this speech. The opposing faction was cowed and silent, French was again bound and returned to his wigwam, where he was received by his friends almost as one risen from the dead.

"But for the mercy of God, moving strangely in a savage's heart, I should indeed now be no longer among the living," said French, still pale and agitated from the fearful strain he had borne. "I understand it not. Thaouvenhosen has been trained in popery by the Jesuit priests, and yet his savage nature seems to show some savor of true Christianity. But for his timely words, my bones ere this would lie blackened in the ashes of the campfire."

# 10

# AN UNEXPECTED PLEASURE

THE next morning, Saturday, March 4th, the Indians were up by early daylight, as was their custom, busily loading their possessions on the sledges, and harnessing the dogs. The dogs were of the Esquimaux breed commonly used in Northern Canada as draft animals. It was hardly strange that the Canadian Indians, according to the Jesuit "Relations," on first seeing horses when imported by the French, called them "big dogs."

The sledges were about nine feet long, rolling up in front, and were made of thin strips of birchwood or oak, held firmly together by thongs of buckskin. A cord of buckskin ran around the edge of the sledge, to which bundles could be lashed. Four dogs, hitched tandem, were attached to each sledge by a harness made also of buckskin. The driver ran behind or beside his team, armed with a long whip, which he did not hesitate to use, keeping his team on a brisk trot or run wherever the going permitted speed. The dogs were of a grayish color, with sharp, pointed noses, and short thick tails curled up over their backs, resembling wolves, some of them being indeed a cross of that animal.

The captives' opinion of these novel teams was well expressed by Ebenezer Nims, who whispered to Stephen and Joseph Kellogg as the boys chanced to stand near him, just before the start:

"Who but savages would think of using dogs to draw loads! It looks like boys' play."

"I know one thing," said Joseph. "If I were at home in Deerfield, and free to go out on the meadow, I would like a team of those dogs of my own to hitch to my sled."

"So would I," said Stephen. "I would like no better sport. But to try really to use them instead of horses or cattle seems silly."

The older white men gazed with still greater contempt on the Indians' rude dog teams as devices well becoming untrained savages. But they were soon to learn that these same savages were far wiser in wilderness craft than them-selves.

These dogs were sinewy and strong. They were capable of drawing two or three hundred pounds, and could travel from twenty to thirty miles a day. They were as hardy as the Indians themselves, and when food was short, capable, like their masters, of subsisting on little or nothing till better days dawned. They needed no roads, and could traverse the wilderness in any direction.

"I thank Thee, O Lord, for Thy tender mercies," cried Mr. Williams in his heart, as, when the procession was ready to start, he saw that several of the youngest children were placed on top the loaded sledges to ride, among them being his own little children, Warham and Eunice. Eunice had been from the first tenderly cared for by her Indian master, who had, in fact, borne the little girl much of the way in his arms. After the contents of many of the packs had been loaded on the sledges, the wounded French and Indians were also placed on board.

The weather had turned colder in the night, and a light sprinkling of snow whitened the river's rough surface over which now set off for the north the long, strange procession of French, Indians, captive men, women, and children, dogs and sledges. They followed the river's great white plain as it wound northward among the towering, pine-clad hills, dark with primeval forest to the top, seeming to frown down forbiddingly on the poor captives below as they travelled on and on into the vast wilderness.

The French went in advance, leaving the captives, as they had from the beginning, wholly to the Indians, taking no notice of them. The English in North America outnumbered the French. Therefore the aid of Indian allies was most important to the French. They well knew if they would retain these fickle allies they must not meddle with that prerogative of war so dear to the Indian heart; the taking and hold-ing of captives. Many of the French were half-breeds, born of Indian mothers, clad like the Indians in buckskin garments and moccasins, hardly to be distinguished in any way from the Indians themselves.

The dogs were urged to their highest speed, and the captives realized how greatly they had underestimated these savage teams when they were forced by their Indian masters to keep up with their progress.

"They travel as if they wanted to kill us all," said Mrs. Nims to Mrs. Belding. Weakened by insufficient food added to their other terrible hardships, the little group of older women dragged themselves along in the rear of the long, straggling procession.

"Little they care," said Mrs. Belding.

"For my part," said Mrs. Carter, "my heart cries out continually, 'How long, O Lord, how long?' I know that ere long I shall go to join my murdered innocents, and truly I would not care how soon but for the four little ones I must leave in their clutches."

"Nor I," said Mrs. Corse. "I am so wearied that to lie down in death would be a blessed rest but for leaving my little Elizabeth alone among the savages."

"We must try still to cling to our faith in God," said Mrs. Brooks. "Our minister is an example to us all. How uncomplainingly he bears his sore afflictions, how he forgets himself in trying to uphold and comfort us."

"Yes," said Mrs. Frary, "to have Mr. Williams with us, though a griev-ous calamity to him, has certainly been a great mercy vouchsafed us."

"God has wondrously strengthened me by his spirit," said young Mrs. Brooks, "for the last encounter with death. I know the end must be near, yet I am not afraid."

"I would I could help you, Mary," said Mrs. Nims. "Your condition of health makes the trial harder for you than for us, even. But it is little we can do for one another now, but to pity one another's sorrows."

Here the women's talk ceased abruptly, for they saw some of the Indians coming back to seek them. Waving their tomahawks over the heads of the little group of pale, suffering women, these fierce masters cried savagely:

"Miserable, good-for-nothing, white squaws. Lag not behind, hop-ing to escape. We will knock you in the head like so many bleating sheep unless you keep up."

The frightened women, summoning all their remaining strength, struggled painfully on, in a vain effort to overtake the main company which was already disappearing around a bend in the river's bank, far ahead.

Stephen Williams, like all the older children, was obliged to walk. The river's surface, rough in many places where floating cakes of ice had jammed together and frozen, hurt his feet, which were tender from long travel in soft moccasins. They grew very sore. The little boy was troubled and frightened. What should he do? It seemed every step he took that he could not take another. But the sun was yet high in the heavens, and nightfall and welcome rest were still weary hours away. He dared not stop to rest a moment, or to loiter, but limped on as fast as he could.

Suddenly Mummumcott turned and came swiftly back towards his little captive. Stephen's heart stood still. Mummumcott was about to kill him, because he was lame!

Oh, the joy, the rebound of relief, when Mummumcott, looking with a sort of grim kindness at the white boy's pitiful, pale face, said:

"Cosannip," for so he had named Stephen, "Cosannip ride now, and rest his sore feet."

Stephen could hardly credit his good fortune, as Mummumcott halted a dog team and told him to mount the load. The relief and the reaction from his terror were so great that he was actually happy for the time. As the four dogs trotted briskly off at a stinging cut from Mummumcott's long whip, Stephen, clinging tightly to the load, bouncing and slipping along over the rough ice, smiled back rapturously at his father, whom he passed, toiling along under a pack.

The father's patient, worn face lit up with a loving smile in return, as he saw his little son's relief and happiness, and his heart swelled with thankfulness to God for another mercy granted in the midst of trouble.

What bliss was Stephen's as he now sat, if not exactly at ease, at least resting his sore, lame feet, borne swiftly along toward the front of the company by his strange team. When he overtook the sledges on which rode Eunice and War-ham, he called to them, but softly, for the Indians allowed no loud talking when journeying:

"See my fine horses, Eunice. See, Warham, my team is trotting right past yours."

"I don't care. My horses are the best horses there is, anyway," piped Warham's baby voice.

"My horses are pretty too," said Eunice. "I am pretending that I am Queen Anne, the great queen in London, riding out in my chariot, drawn by four cream-colored horses."

"I wouldn't care about being the queen," said Stephen. "I'm Governor Dudley and his court, going forth to the hunt out of Boston. I shall kill bears and deer and wolves a plenty as I ride along."

Perhaps this fancy occurred to him because he noticed all around in the fresh, light snow coating the river's ice the records of their doings plainly written by wild beast and bird. Countless tracks of wolves and foxes, and of deer hoofs delicately imprinted, crossed and interlaced on the river's snowy plain. The trail of rabbits and the tracks of birds' feet, criss-crossing, also made a pretty network of delicate patterns.

Stephen amused himself by holding his arms up and pointing an imaginary gun at the game he pictured all around him, saying softly:

"Bang!"

Mummumcott, as he ran beside the sledge, looked pleased. He thought the white boy a lad of spirit, and that he could rear him to be a real Indian hunter and warrior. He said:

"When we come to the winter hunting-ground, Mummumcott will make Cosannip a little bow and arrow such as his Indian brothers carry. Then Cosannip can shoot squirrels and birds and, maybe, a wild-cat."

Stephen wished that Esther could ride too. And, by and by, he saw her allowed to take a turn in riding. The Indians were merciful to the children and younger prisoners, perhaps because they hoped to swell their tribal numbers, sadly diminished in constant wars, by adopting them, and rearing them to be, not only genuine savages in all their habits and thoughts, but also good Roman Catholics. To save the souls of the English captives by their conversion was a duty constantly impressed by their Jesuit fathers. Moreover, the Indians were naturally fond of children and indulgent to them.

But for the older women they had no mercy. There could be little hope of changing either their habits or their faith. If any became too worn to travel, they were calmly slain, with as little feeling as though they had been domestic animals.

So it fell out that, near the end of this longest and hardest day of all this mournful journey, as Mrs. Carter, Mrs. Frary, Mrs. Nims, and Mrs. French lagged farther and farther behind, in spite of their utmost efforts to drag themselves along, their Indian masters killed them all, tearing off their scalps, and going on, as if the incident were of trifling importance.

The bleeding bodies of the good Deerfield women lay on the river's ice, in the dreary solitude, the prey of wild beast and bird; but their souls, unconscious of the brief agony of dying, had entered into the great peace.

Ruth Catlin, though a delicate girl, had been from the first upborne by her high spirit. She walked off with such elasticity and endurance, scorning to complain, or even show fatigue if she could help it, that her Indian master, treating her as he would his squaw had she been in the company, took a part of his own pack and loaded it on her shoulders.

"Poor Ruth! Is it not a cruel shame?" whispered Sarah Hoyt to Ebenezer Nims, who, somehow, often contrived to walk near Sarah, aiding her whenever he could. It was a help to Sarah to have the sympathy and companionship of this friend from childhood, to know that Ebenezer cared. Often Deacon Hoyt was unable to speak to his daughter for a whole day, as usually they were separated far apart in the company.

Ebenezer did not yet know of his mother's cruel death. She had been so far behind that he had not seen her since the start in the early morning; and his master would not allow him to go back to her aid, as Ebenezer had begged to do. Not until they camped at night, and it was found that the four women who had been slain came no more, would their friends know what their fate had been.

"These Indians seem to have no more feelings of compassion than so many wild beasts," said Ebenezer, little dreaming what fresh cause he would soon have for this opinion. "But I am glad, Sallie, that sometimes they let me help you on."

"So am I, Eben," said Sarah, simply.

When John Catlin saw his delicate, pretty sister bending under her load, he felt the sight more than he could bear. He whispered to her:

"Gladly would I carry that load for you, Ruth, were I not so heavily laden already that I can hardly struggle along."

"You have enough to do, to bear your part, John," said Ruth. "I would our dear mother could see how wonderfully you have held out. I dare say she worries not a little about you."

As has been said, John Catlin was not strong, and had never slept from under his father's roof until dragged away on this terrible jaunt to Canada.

"I care not for myself so much," said John. "A man can stand a good deal, if he has to. But to put such burdens on a girl! It kills me to see you a slave to savages, sister."

"I am no slave to them, as I'll show you," said Ruth. With a spirited flash of her black eyes she threw her burden off and down on the ice, as far back as her strength could toss it, marching on unburdened, her head defiantly held high.

"Ruth!" exclaimed her brother, in dismay. "Are you crazy? They will slay you!"

"I am not afraid of them," said Ruth.

To John's amazement, Ruth's master, instead of burying his hatchet in her head then and there, as John fully expected, laughed and seemed pleased with his captive's spirit. He went back, picked up her load, and added it to his own, and Ruth walked on unincumbered.

"He treats you as if you were a princess," said John that night, as he saw how her master brought Ruth plenty of food, and the best to be obtained. John, like many others among the captives, had nothing, save as Ruth divided her share with him.

"'Tis because I am not afraid of him," said Ruth. "I loathe the Indians so much I can't fear them. I simply despise them."

Another captive who had been wonderfully sustained was young Hannah Sheldon. Spraining her ankle before setting forth on such a dreadful journey, her friends had feared that she would be one of the first to fall by the way. But the same indomitable spirit that had brought her a bride to take up her abode at Deerfield in such dangerous times now buoyed up the body, as spirit can.

Hannah had continued somehow to keep on and up, and when some friend pitied her, she said with indomitable courage:

"I know that I shall reach Canada alive, and I know too that John will soon see that I am redeemed."

By night the company had reached the mouth of a small river. Here more substantial wigwams than usual were erected, as if for a longer halt than that ordinarily made. The dogs were unhitched, and soon were stretched out around the camp-fires blazing high. The blue smoke curling up through the openings in the wigwam tops was the only smoke rising for many miles around in all that northern wilderness.

# 11

# SUNDAY IN THE WILDERNESS

MR. WILLIAMS had rarely been so surprised in his life, rich in varied experiences, as when his master Suckkeecoo said to him that night:

"Tomorrow is the Sabbath."

"Full well do I know that," said Mr. Williams with a heavy sigh, thinking how only a week ago he had stood in his own pulpit, preaching to, alas, how many now numbered with the dead.

"A sorry Lord's day this for me and my flock," he thought, but did not say.

"The army rests here over the Sabbath. The Christian Indians," continued Suckkeecoo, not noticing Mr. Williams's involuntary expression of utter astonishment at the, to him, novel idea of "Christian" Indians,—"the Christian Indians command the English priest to pray after his fashion tomorrow."

"Most gladly will I do so," said Mr. Williams, his face brightening, though he could not overcome his wonder at this strange and unexpected invitation to preach.

Later, as he had opportunity, he cheered the hearts of the captives— doubly dejected tonight, as the disappearance of their four friends told the mournful story of their fate—with the glad tidings of this day's rest and the religious service to be held by him.

"Could my poor Mary but have held out a little longer this day's rest might have saved her life," said Thomas French, his face drawn with grief.

"'Tis surely a great mercy God has granted us in our desolate condition," said Deacon Hoyt. "Only He could have moved the Indians' hearts so to relent."

"In truth, I think the French and Indians themselves feel the need of a rest, after the killing pace we have kept up ever since we left Deerfield," said Stebbins. "'Tis a wonder to me, not that so many have given out along the way, but rather that any of our women and children are still living. To rest one day, and to hear the familiar voice of our good minister uplifted once more in religious service, will greatly revive our fainting spirits."

"If Mary could only have held out till tonight," murmured Thomas French.

Never was seen a stranger Sunday's service than that held next day by Mr. Williams at the mouth of Williams River, on the banks of the Connecticut. In the centre of the space among the wigwams blazed a huge camp-fire. Seated around it, on logs, skins, or packs, or standing in little groups, were the sorrowful captives, their faces wasted and pale from suffering already endured, and the constant apprehension of unknown horrors yet to come ever attending them. Many of them also had been stricken to the heart by the cruel slaughter of some dear one during the march.

Mingled among them were many of their Indian masters, their red skins, thick black hair, and gleaming black eyes giving their white captives a curiously faded look by contrast. Not only did they wish to keep vigilant watch over these captives, but they were also curious to hear what the English priest would say.

The French soldiers, as usual, were encamped by themselves at some distance from their Indian allies. But from idleness and curiosity some of them also joined the motley congregation of Mr. Williams. Their dress was a mixture of French uniform and the rude skin habit of the coureurs des bois, the plumes that nodded here and there from an officer's head shading faces bronzed by constant exposure to a dark hue rivaling that of the Indians.

If the congregation was unusual, so was the church. A snow storm during the night had turned into hail and rain, clearing towards morning with a cold wind that had frozen all into a glittering crust. The white plain of the Connecticut shone like a sheet of dazzling silver, and it was almost impossible to look at the glistening hills around, so brilliantly did they gleam in the bright sunlight. The shadows of every tree trunk were reflected in the crust as in a mirror, and every twig and branch of every tree was clad in icy mail, tinkling faintly as the wind clashed them together. Even the dead weeds and seed stalks of the goldenrod, standing up through the snow, were beautiful as they glittered in the sun, and cast their delicate fretwork of shadows on the crust below.

The church was most beautiful, and spoke more plainly of its Divine Architect than does many a costly cathedral. But the hearts of the captives were too heavy within them to feel its beauty. They were only sensible of their own exceeding misery, as they waited anxiously for some uplifting word of comfort from their minister, which might perhaps give them courage to bear on.

Mr. Williams stood in the centre of this motley company under the open sky, clad in his Indian garment of deerskin and fringed leggings, his head bare. His heart thrilled within him, as he gazed around a moment before beginning on this sorrowful company of his old Deerfield parishioners,' feeling the silent appeal for help in the eyes fixed on him so intently, and he cried in his heart:

"Help me, O Heavenly Father, to speak some comfortable word of Thy truth to sustain these Thy sorely afflicted children!"

He read the Forty-second Psalm, and other comforting passages from the small copy of the Bible he had managed to bring from home even in the stress of such a departure, and prayed with a fervor never heard in the home pulpit.

When he cried, "Save us and sustain us, O God, for Thou only canst help, to Thee only can we look," the words were not mere words, as they might perchance have been in the Sunday service if safely at home, but were vital with deep meaning for every hearer.

He took for his text Lamentations, first chapter and eighteenth verse: "The Lord is righteous; for I have rebelled against His commandment: hear, I pray you, all people, and behold my sorrow: my virgins and my young men are gone into captivity."

The attention of the children was somewhat distracted from the sermon by the dogs, who, lying stretched around the fire in luxurious ease, fell to snapping and snarling at each other, until Mummumcott settled all differences by dispersing them with his long whip. But the older captives had neither eyes nor ears for anything but their minister and his words. If only they could get some help to endure!

When Mr. Williams ended his sermon, Oioteet said:

"Now the English must sing in their manner. Let them shout aloud the praises of their God in song."

"They that carry us away captive require of us one of the songs of Zion," said Mr. Williams, turning towards the captives. "Let us unite in singing the Nineteenth Psalm, whose words are so familiar to you."

The voices of the captives, weakened by fasting and weariness, rose but feebly and quaveringly on the wintry air. Some among them wiped away furtive tears as the familiar words, full of tender associations with happier days and vanished friends, rose among such strange, forbidding surroundings. But they sang on:

"The heavens and the fyrmamente,
Do wondrously declare,
The glory of God omnipotent,
His works and what they are.
"Each day declareth by his course
An other daye to come;
And by the night we know lykwise
A nightly course to run.
"In them the Lord made royally
A settle for the sunne,
Where like a Gyant joyfully
He myght his journey runne."

Oioteet here broke in contemptuously:

"The singing of the English is like the squeaking of mice. Indian papooses make a louder noise."

"Their God could not hear their song, were He only in the treetop," said Masseamet. "When the Indians sing, the great noise rises to the sky overhead, the Great Spirit hears it in his home in the sun, the eagle high on his rock trembles at the mighty sound, and the wild bear and the hungry wolf hide themselves."

"The Indians would be better pleased with 'The Forefathers' Song,'" whispered Joseph Kellogg to Stephen. "That rolls forth more jovially than a psalm."

"But you know, Joseph," said Stephen, "that my father would never countenance breaking the Sabbath by singing a worldly song on that day."

"No, of course he wouldn't, usually," said Joseph. "I would not think of such a thing at home in Deerfield. But perhaps now, to please our Indian masters, he might suffer it."

"No," said Stephen, who well knew his father's unflinching steadfastness to what he thought right, "he never would, not even to save his life, I believe, because, you see, Joseph, it would be a sin."

Mr. Williams improved the leisure of this day to talk with his own children and others, exhorting them to stand fast in the true faith, the faith of their fathers, amid all coming temptations and dangers, when they might be separated far from him. He especially feared for his children and flock the exposure to arguments and influence in behalf of Catholicism, which he knew surely awaited them in Canada. Puritan and Jesuit, each equally earnest in serving God after the fashion which they felt to be the only truth, were equally firm in the belief that the opposing faith was devil born. The first Christian duty was to spare no effort to save the souls holding such erroneous views, and redeem them at all costs to the true faith.

After the service, the Indians scattered about hunting for game, which was not plentiful, a few only remaining in camp to guard the captives. For the latter, the day, if far enough from being happy or comfortable, was at least a welcome rest, and likely to impart some fresh strength for the travels of the coming week.

# 12

# A FALSE ALARM

EARLY Monday morning the camp was broken up and the dreary march northward resumed.

Stephen heard Mummumcott say sneeringly to Deacon Hoyt, as he saw that good man looking longingly back to the south, towards the old home, from which he must now go still farther away:

"The Englishman will need eagle's eyes if he look to see an army of his people coming to rescue him. The English tremble before the Indians. They dare not venture to follow our trail, for they know we will drink their blood like water, and take the scalps from their heads to trim our garments. When the rabbit chases the wolf, then will the English pursue the Indians."

Deacon Hoyt heaved a patient sigh and made no answer. Well he knew that the hope of rescue was faint, and yet hope, so hard to kill, whispered; perchance troops might have come up from below to Deerfield and be even now close behind. If the good God would only permit their rescue!

Some such feeling he expressed to Mr. Williams as the two chanced to walk together for a while, near the front of the long procession.

"God's mercy is great, and His power boundless," said Mr Williams in reply. "Perchance He may yet see it best to vouchsafe our release and return to our pleasant valley. But His ways are past our comprehension, and we must still trust in Him, e'en though His will and not ours be done."

At that instant, all were startled by a rapid firing of muskets, far back in the rear. Instantly the Indians were in commotion.

"The English army is upon us," they cried. "Bind the captives and make ready for battle."

Eager hope flushed the captives' worn faces, even though their hands were bound, none too gently, behind their backs, and they were driven like a flock of helpless sheep into a wooded ravine. Here a guard of Indians stood over them with hatchets, war clubs, and loaded guns, saying that all captives should be slain before they would be surrendered to the English.

The main body of the Indians hastily took vantage points behind trees and rocks, ready to shoot down the enemy without exposing their own persons. But soon they were relieved by learning that this alarm was needless. The firing had come from some of their own number in the rear of the company, who, in the shortness of provision, could not resist the temptation to shoot at a flock of wild-geese flying high overhead, bound for their northern summer haunts.

In spite of all their professions of scorn for the English, the Indians were evidently delighted when this alarm proved to be a false one. They shot off volleys for joy, the sharp reports echoing wildly from the hills around, and said boastfully:

"It is as we said. The English fear the Indians. Well do they know that the Indian's heart is stout, his eye keen, his knife sharp, and that he will spring on the English like the panther when they little look for him. The English tremble at our name. They are afraid to follow us."

The hearts of the poor captives sank into more dreary dejection after this momentary gleam of hope, as they again marched on in the same fashion as on previous days, traveling farther this day, after the Sunday's rest, than on any day before.

The rapid pace told on Mr. Williams, whose injured ankle again grew very lame. Stephen overtook him as he hobbled feebly on.

"My son," said his father, "perchance I have but a short time to be with you. My lameness has so increased that I fear I cannot travel much farther. I may soon be slain."

"O father!" cried Stephen, tears rushing to his eyes as he seized his father's hand. Must he lose father as well as mother in this same cruel manner, and be left a helpless orphan in the hands of their murderers?

"Hush, Stephen," said his father. "Yield not to your grief, lest you anger the Indians. And listen to me, for I may have but a moment in which to talk to you. If you live to reach Canada, make known who you are, a son of the minister of Deerfield, and you may receive kinder treatment. Above all, my son, stand fast, amid all temptations and troubles, to the faith of your fathers. Let no—"

Here Mummumcott came and took Stephen away, jealous of his father's talk and influence. The terrified boy, trembling for his dear father, often strained his eyes, looking back to the rear of the company, where Mr. Williams's lameness now forced him to walk, to see if he were still alive. Not until the company went into camp at night near the foot of a great mountain *(Mt. Ascutney)* was his terrible anxiety at last relieved by seeing his father come limping in, the last of the procession. He begged Mummumcott to allow him to speak to his father, and Mummumcott said:

"Cosannip must be an Indian now. Not think about his white father. Go for one minute."

Stephen cared not what Mummumcott said, so long as he gave him permission to be with his father, even for a moment. He ran eagerly to the spot where Mr. Williams, weak as he was, stood bent under the burden of a heavy pack fastened on his back.

"Let me help you, father," cried Stephen. "I can undo the straps. Oh, how glad I am that you were not slain! I trembled, every strange sound I heard."

"God was pleased to strengthen me, miraculously, as it seemed, to perform my journey," said Mr. Williams, sinking down on a fallen tree trunk. Oh, how welcome was merely the privilege of stopping and sitting quietly down, after the day's hard, incessant travel!

The other children, too, were allowed to be with their father for a short time. It seemed so good, so natural to them to be near their father. To feel that much of the old home love was an unspeakable comfort in their dreary surroundings. To hear his voice, to feel his tender love,—ah, how precious it was!

"I feel undeserving of God's great mercy manifested towards me," said Mr. Williams, "when I see others called to suffer so sorely. I had the anguish to-day of seeing two more of the good women of my flock mercilessly slain, because so faint they could no longer travel; Mrs. Belding and Mrs. Corse; and Mary Brooks will soon give out, I fear. Truly, my flock has become a flock of slaughter. They are driven like lambs to the shambles."

The next morning the great mountain beneath whose shadow they had encamped was shrouded from view by a driving snow storm. The weather was bitterly cold. Yet, in spite of cold and storm, the tramp to the north must be resumed.

In the early dawn the entrance to the wigwam in which Mr. Williams had slept was darkened by some one entering. Looking up, to his surprise he saw Mrs. Brooks tottering in, hardly able to stand. She was one of the most devout among the younger women in his church, and Mr. Williams was deeply attached to her. He said tenderly:

"Mary, my poor child, I am sorry to see you in such a pitiful condition. Why do you come so early?"

"God," said Mrs. Brooks, "has inclined the heart of my master to let me come and take my last farewell of you, my dear pastor and friend. By repeated falls on the ice yesterday, I so injured myself that I can go no farther. I know I shall be slain today."

Mr. Williams grasped her hand, with an exclamation of pity and horror.

"I bless God," continued Mrs. Brooks, eagerly making the most of the brief time allowed her, "that He has strengthened me for my last encounter with death. Many passages of scripture have come into my mind, as if sent from above to aid me. I am not afraid of death. God has given me grace cheerfully to submit to His will."

Here her Indian master appeared with frowning face, roughly seizing and dragging her away.

"Pray for me, that God may take me to Himself," said Mrs. Brooks, as she was dragged out of the wigwam.

"I will, poor child," said Mr. Williams. "Think much on the Saviour's sufferings, Mary. May He sustain thee!"

The company had not marched far in the storm when Mary Brooks's forebodings were realized, and she was added to the list of murdered women and children whose bodies lay beside the long trail stretching back to far-away Deerfield.

As the company toiled on along the surface of the frozen river in the teeth of the storm, which drove furiously in their faces and covered their bodies with shaggy whiteness, Stephen Williams grew so cold that he said to his brother Samuel, when he had a chance to speak to him:

"Sam, I really believe I shall freeze. I never was so cold."

"Does not the toilsome walking make your blood stir?" asked Samuel. "I too was cold when we started,—we have so little food, 't is no wonder we are cold,—but now toiling along through this deep snow against the storm and wind, I feel fairly warm again."

"I don't," said Stephen. "I grow colder and colder. One of my feet aches with cold."

"Stamp it hard," said Samuel. "Perhaps that will set the blood circulating."

"I dare not stamp or do anything," said Stephen, "lest I fall behind and be slain, as poor Mrs. Brooks was a little while ago. Did you have any breakfast, Sam?"

"Yes, I suppose you would call it so. I had the leg of a wild-goose that my master was so lucky as to kill yesterday," said Sam. "I waited for no cooking, but devoured it raw, to the last scrap. I believe I could have eaten feathers and all, I am so starved. I hope you had better fare Stephen "

"No, I only had three kernels of parched corn," said Stephen. "Mummumcott has still left in his pouch a little of this corn which he brought from Canada. I guess that is one reason I am so cold, because I am so faint with hunger "

"Some of the folks had not a morsel to eat last night, after walking all day," said Samuel. "I wonder that we bear it as well as we do."

That night the company reached the mouth of another small river, what is now White River, in Hartford Vt. After the wigwams had been erected, Mummumcott, who, as Stephen grew lamer and lamer, had noticed the difficulty the boy had in walking, took him by the fire in their wigwam, and pulled off his moccasins and the remains of the woolen socks which Stephen still wore, knit by the hands of his good mother. The little feet were pallid and cold.

Mummumcott pinched Stephen's feet. Stephen cried out as the first foot was pinched, but the second had no feeling. It was numb, and the great-toe badly frozen.

"Huh," grunted Mummumcott, not pleased to have his captive thus disabled. He rubbed the foot roughly with handfuls of snow, until at last it grew red, and Stephen cried out with pain.

"Huh," grunted Mummumcott again, this time with satisfaction. He wrapped the aching foot up in a rabbit's skin, the fur inside, which felt comforting to Stephen. He was given a few grains of corn for his supper, and then allowed to lie down by the fire. The warmth and repose were so grateful to the exhausted boy that he soon forgot his troubles in a deep sleep.

From a happy dream of the old home and mother, he was rudely wakened by Mummumcott shaking him.

"Wake up, Cosannip," said Mummumcott. "Cosannip must come down to the great river at once."

Stephen, confused and startled, hardly realizing at first his surroundings, was frightened at this unusual order. Was Mummumcott going to kill him because his foot was disabled?

In the gray, chilly light of early dawn, Stephen hobbled down to the shore of the Connecticut. There stood Mummumcott, pack on his back, as if ready for travelling, and with him was an Indian lad a little older than Stephen, named Kewakcum, who had been with the party left behind at West River to guard the dogs and sledges during the attack on Deerfield. Stephen knew that Kewakcum was a nephew of Mummumcott, but in the large, mixed company had not been as yet thrown much with him.

Kewakcum stood with his bright, bead-like eyes fixed in curiosity on the little pale-faced boy, who, roused so hastily, stood shivering, partly with cold, partly with nervous fear, as he gazed piteously on Mummumcott, who only said:

"Come on now. Mummumcott goes to his own hunting-ground."

Kewakcum bore a small pack, and Mummumcott proceeded to bind a still smaller one on Stephen's back. Stephen looked about bewildered. The camp was all quiet. No one else seemed stirring yet.

"But the others? My father and the rest?" he ventured to say.

"Game is scarce for so many," said Mummumcott. "The Indians scatter here, to seek different hunting-grounds. Mummumcott goes to his wigwam and family. Cosannip is his, and goes with him."

Having deigned this explanation, Mummumcott strode away up the river, followed by Kewakcum, and by Stephen, who dared not object or delay. The dog sledge hitherto driven by Mummumcott belonged to some of the Canadian Indians, and so must now be left behind. Again the packs must all be carried.

Stephen limped away behind the two Indians, casting wistful glances back at the silent cluster of wigwams from which a faint smoke curled up, until a turn in the river hid them from view.

Should he never see again his dear father, his brothers and sisters? Must he indeed go away alone among the Indians, and become one himself, as Mummumcott had said? How would his father feel when he woke and found that his boy had vanished, he knew not where?

Such were Stephen's sad thoughts as he walked behind his companions.

# 13

# ALONE WITH THE INDIANS

THE Indians who had assaulted Deerfield being now so distant from that place felt it safe to break up into small parties and scatter about for better opportunities in hunting. It was impossible at this season to secure game enough in any one locality to feed so large a party. The French of the army went off by themselves, leaving the Indians to their own pleasure. Part of the Indians were going to take that path to Canada, so sadly familiar to English captives, up the White River to its sources, over the Green Mountains, across the short divide to the head-waters of the Winooski, down that stream to Lake Champlain, and thence to Canada. This was the road Mr. Williams, his remaining children, and most of the Deerfield captives were destined to travel. But little Stephen, only ten years old, was, as we have seen, borne away by his Indian master to dwell among the Indians, and be, so far as they could make him, a genuine Indian boy.

Not a morsel to eat had Stephen that morning, or indeed all day. But at least Mummumcott was only inflicting on his little captive hardships shared by himself and his nephew. Neither of them had tasted food that morning. Mummumcott still had in his pouch a little parched corn, but that must be carefully hoarded against the imminent danger of absolute starvation, should he continue to have ill luck in hunting.

The three walked steadily on, the Indians in their habitual silence, and Stephen following mutely in their tracks, keeping up as well as his lameness permitted. He said nothing. There was nothing for him to say, and he was too faint and depressed to talk. He must save all his strength and bend every energy simply to keeping up with his companions, who strode straight on, evidently as much at home in the wilderness as any citizen in his own streets.

Mummumcott kept a vigilant eye out for possible game. But yesterday's storm had effaced all the old tracks, and he found few fresh ones, and none which led to any success.

They walked until about nine o'clock in the evening as Stephen judged it to be, before they stopped for the night Stephen thought they had walked forty miles since morning. How long ago seemed even yesterday, when he had his father, brothers, and sisters! How far away seemed the camp where he had left them all! As for the old home life in Deer-field, it seemed like a dream,—something too happy and delightful to have been true.

Mummumcott now gave Stephen and Kewakcum each a spoonful of the precious parched corn, the first food they had tasted that day. Even this seemed a mercy to Stephen, in his faintness.

As he rolled himself up in the deerskin which was part of the pack he carried, and lay down for the night, like the Indians, with his feet to the fire, the religious ideas so carefully instilled by his father were his only comfort, but yet a help very real and precious.

"I must not forget now what father has always told me," thought the boy. "God is here. He can see me now, just as plainly as if I were at home in my own bed in Deerfield."

Stephen could not help crying a little at this thought, as a vivid memory of the old home love came over him. But he bravely repressed his grief, thinking:

"I must not cry. It does no good. Now I will thank God for His care of me to-day. But for that I could never have kept up on such a long walk when so lame."

Exhausted as he was, Stephen thanked his Heavenly Father with real gratitude for His care that day, and besought His help and protection for the morrow and all the days to come. Then, comforted a little in his loneliness, he fell into the heavy slumber of utter exhaustion.

In the morning, Mummumcott dealt out to each five or six kernels of corn from his scanty hoard. This was the breakfast on which they must travel.

As Stephen walked on, he found himself involuntarily thinking about johnny-cake and sausage, and hot biscuits dripping with fresh butter, and baked pork and beans, until he could almost have declared that he smelled these good things, steaming hot from the big brick oven.

"And even bread and milk," he thought. "How I would like some of Parthena's light bread, crumbled into a nice porringer of sweet, rich milk! And to think that sometimes I used to be willful, and find fault with my supper, and say I was tired of plain bread and milk! Perhaps it may be because I sinned thus that I perish with hunger now."

He tried in vain to banish from his mind these tantalizing visions of tempting food, knowing that they only aggravated his hunger, and made it harder to bear.

About noon, as Stephen knew by the height of the heavens, Mummumcott abandoned the Connecticut River on which they had travelled thus far, and took to its west shore. Later in the afternoon the monotony of the trackless wilderness—where on every side were only to be seen rocks and trees, wild mountain ranges, snow and ice—was broken, to Stephen's joy, by the welcome sight of two wigwams in the distance.

"Here, maybe, we shall get something to eat," thought Stephen, with lively hopes.

"Ho, ho," called Mummumcott, evidently expecting to find friends here, as he confidently approached the wigwams.

No answering call came; no one appeared. No smoke ascended from the wigwams. They were deserted, although there were many signs of recent occupation. A few red embers still glowed faintly in the heap of ashes in the wigwam's centre.

"Go into the wigwams and stay," commanded Mummumcott, as he deposited his own pack on the ground, and taking his gun, added, "Mummumcott goes to track the moose."

The two boys, the red-skinned Kewakcum and the fair-haired Stephen, thus left to their own devices, first rid them-selves of their packs. Then Kewakcum proceeded to rekindle the expiring fire. Under the wigwam's slanting edge he found some dry branches and rotten wood stored. These soon kindled, as Kewakcum blew up the embers, fanning them with his deerskin coat. The cheerful blaze lit up the rude interior, putting a better face on things at once, and the warmth was most grateful to the famished boys.

"Good. Heap good fire," said Kewakcum, looking at Stephen with the friendly smile of one boy comrade for another.

"Yes. It is grand," said Stephen, smiling back, as he rubbed his cold hands over the blaze. In his forlorn state he was ready to meet any friendly advances.

"Now," said Kewakcum, "we must hunt for food. Maybe our brothers have hid some here. Cosannip hunt this wigwam over, Kewakcum look in the other. See what we find.

Stephen made a thorough search, pulling about the piles of pine and hemlock branches used for beds, and ransacking all the debris left in the wigwam by its former occupants, but nothing could he find.

Presently he heard from the other wigwam a joyous cry, "Ho, ho." He ran eagerly out and met Kewakcum.

"What is it? What did you find?" cried Stephen eagerly.

Kewakcum waved aloft in one hand a handful of bones, holding in the other the paunch of a moose.

"Our brothers killed a moose; maybe many moose. Maybe buried the meat in the snow near by. Cosannip and Kewakcum hunt it up."

First, before the hungry boys went a step farther, they gnawed eagerly at these poor bones, but the few shreds of flesh still clinging to them were too hard and dry to yield even to the boys' sharp young teeth. The effort was only an aggravation.

Kewakcum made Stephen understand that it was a custom of Indian hunters, when they had the good fortune to kill several moose, to bury the meat they could not then eat near by the camp in the snow for future use.

"We go hunt it," said Kewakcum, with bright eyes. "Kewakcum go this way, towards the north star, Cosannip that way," pointing south. "Good supper by and by, maybe. Roast moose meat fills Cosannip's stomach."

Stephen, animated by joy at this bright hope, set bravely forth into the forest south of the wigwams. He had become by this time so accustomed to snow-shoes that he was able to walk over the deep drifts in the woods between the tall trees without much difficulty, except as his lame foot still hampered him. He found a long, stout, fallen branch, broken off in a high wind, and with this for a staff he made good progress.

Eagerly he scanned the aisles of the forest, this side and that, for any signs of a place where the Indians might possibly have buried their precious store of meat. Many a mound of snow did he dig into with his pointed staff, to find it only a mound of snow, and nothing more, the ground beneath frozen hard and undisturbed. Under the low drooping branches of hemlocks he pried anxiously, and into gullies in the rocks he wandered, but all in vain. Nothing could he find.

So absorbed in this search was he that he hardly realized how tired he was growing. But at last, as still he found nothing, he began to feel his exhaustion.

"I must go back to the wigwam," he thought. "Indians have sharper eyes than white folks. I guess Kewakcum will have better luck than 1. 1 hope so, anyway."

But now a new trouble awaited him. He had wandered so far in the pathless woods, where one tree looked much like another to him, that he had not even the least idea in which direction to turn to find the wigwams. He was hopelessly bewildered and lost!

A horrible fear possessed him.

"What if I never find my way back! Then I must he down here in the woods and starve to death,—it will not take long,—or be eaten up by some hungry wild beast!"

In his terror the boy ran as fast as his clumsy snow-shoes allowed, now this way, now that, among the great trees. In his haste he stumbled over a prostrate tree trunk half hidden in the snow, and fell headlong into a drift, managing to scramble out and up only after some time and with greatest difficulty.

He stopped to listen, if perchance by good fortune he might hear Kewakcum. Through the aisles of the forest he peered anxiously in every direction, but nothing stirred, save branches tossed by the wind. He seemed the only living creature moving in all that vast solitude. The awesome stillness frightened him. There was no sound, save the creaking of a branch and the wind sighing solemnly through the dark pine boughs overhanging him, a mournful sound, as if even the great pines pitied the lost boy. He was so small, and the wild forest around so vast!

Suddenly the silence was broken by the distant sound of footsteps drawing nearer. Even Stephen's unpracticed ears told him that these were not the steps of a man.

"Maybe some wild animal is coming to devour me," thought Stephen. "O God, Thou canst see! Help and save me now, I pray thee!"

The steps came nearer, as Stephen stood still with dread. A great heavy animal came floundering through the snow, thrusting its big head, heavy with its fat nose and clumsy horns, through the thick pine branches. Stephen knew it was a moose. Relieved as he was, he could not help wishing:

"Oh, if I were only a man and had a gun!"

The moment the moose's eyes fell on Stephen, wildly terrified, it veered off, and fled, plunging along more swiftly through the snow and among the trees.

Again Stephen was alone.

"What shall I do?" he thought. "By and by the sun will set. It will be dark and I shall soon freeze. I must shout as loud as I can, and see if I cannot make Kewakcum come."

"Kewakcum! Kewakcum!" shouted Stephen, with all the force he could put into his boyish voice. "Hallo! Hallo! Help! Help! Kewakcum, come! Kewakcum!"

His voice sounded strange and unnatural to him, as it resounded through the silent forest, waking an echo against some distant hill, which shouted back mysteriously from afar:

"Kewakcum! Kewakcum!"

It frightened and awed Stephen, as he heard this solemn voice of the forest. But, after waiting a while, listening for an answering hallo from Kewakcum, he, in desperation, renewed his shouts more vigorously than before.

Now, listening again, he heard some one or something coming, he knew not what. He stood still, waiting with fast-beating heart.

Then out from behind a tree strode his master, Mummumcott. His dark red face wore a savage scowl, and he rushed upon Stephen, the breach of his gun raised, as if to dash out his brains.

"Hush, little fool," he said. "Have you no sense? I will soon stop your noise. I will kill you."

Stephen cowered before the enraged Indian, as the gun was brandished fiercely over his head, thinking that now the end had surely come. But Mummumcott presently controlled his anger. The white captive would be useful to him hereafter. He would let him live, and try to teach him the manners of the forest.

Seeing his face relent, as the hand with the gun fell by his side, Stephen, who would have cried had he dared, said piteously:

"Cosannip is lost. Good Mummumcott, please show me the way back to the wigwam."

"Follow me," said Mummumcott, striding off through the forest with unerring instinct, straight to the wigwams.

As they walked, he tutored Stephen.

"If Cosannip wants to be an Indian brave, he must learn Indian wisdom. Indians know much. Indians never hollo in the woods. Only fools and Englishmen hollo in the woods. Loud noise puts enemy on the Indian's track, scares the game. The Indian glides through the forest, slipping along as still as his grandfather, the rattlesnake. For a signal to his brother, he barks like the fox, howls like the wolf, hoots like the owl, chirps like the bird. Cosannip must learn to talk like the animals."

When they reached the wigwams, Mummumcott said:

"Cosannip stay here, and bid Kewakcum stay here, till Mummumcott comes again. Mummumcott goes now to track the moose Cosannip frightened by his papoose cries."

Thus saying, Mummumcott departed, swiftly and silently, on the track whence they had come. Stephen, left alone, was so thankful to be rescued and safe that it seemed a sort of happiness merely to be back in the shelter of the deserted wigwam. The fire was getting low, so he went out and gathered armfuls of fallen branches to replenish it. There was at least some comfort in its warmth and brightness.

After a while, Kewakcum returned, but, alas! empty handed.

"No moose meat," he said, shaking his head sadly. "Guess Indians much hungry. Eat moose meat all up. But Kewakcum will cook some supper."

"How can you cook supper when there is nothing to cook and no vessel to cook in?" asked Stephen in wonder.

"Cosannip will see. Indians heap wise," said Kewakcum.

Stephen watched Kewakcum's doings with lively interest, as first he took the moose's paunch outside the wigwam, slashed it open with a knife he carried in a sheath hanging at his belt, a knife made of a sharp-pointed stone lashed firmly into a split stick by means of a stout deerskin thong tied tightly around this handle. He scraped the skin with the same knife, and then rubbed it clean with snow.

He had already raked open the fire, exposing a glowing bed of coals. Under these coals he had thrust several small round stones that Stephen had noticed lying on the ground near the fire.

Kewakcum now brought from his pack a vessel made of birch bark sewed tightly together. He filled this with water from a brook not far away, and dropped the stones, when hot, into this water, soon heating it. Then he put the bones, after he had carefully cracked them open, and the paunch skin, into the vessel, and dropped in more hot stones.

Soon, to Stephen's surprise, his nose, keen with hunger, began to detect a meaty odor. Or was it only his hungry fancy?

When Kewakcum considered the broth done, he brought from his pack two small bowls, made like the larger vessel of birch bark. Stephen, meantime, was watching him eagerly.

"Come, Cosannip, come and eat," said Kewakcum, as he handed Stephen one of the little bowls with quite the gracious air of a grown warrior inviting a comrade to a feast.

The boiling water had softened the sinews and dried flesh still clinging to the bones, and drawn out the marrow (for which purpose Kewakcum had cracked open the bones), and there really was some taste of meat to this broth, which both boys drank eagerly. It was hot and comforting, and relieved, somewhat, their desperate faintness.

This supper over, Kewakcum bade Stephen come out into the woods with him. Both brought back a big backload of wood and branches to be ready for the morning fire. Then Kewakcum buried the bed of coals deep in ashes, to hold the fire over night.

Mummumcott did not appear again that night. The two boys lay down alone on their bed of branches, in their solitary wigwam, their moccasins under their heads, their feet in the warm ashes, their bodies wrapped tight in skins, the fur inside.

Ere the weary Stephen fell asleep, he did not forget to thank God for all the mercies shown him that day. In such prayer lay his only comfort and hope.

# 14

# FARTHER ON

WHEN Stephen awoke next morning, he found himself alone
in the wigwam. Kewakcum was nowhere to be seen. The fire
had recently been replenished with green wood, which made a dense
smoke, causing Stephen's eyes to smart, as he sat up, rubbing them,
and looking dolefully around. Oh, how faint and empty he felt!

"What if Kewakcum has deserted me, and gone off, leaving me here
alone in the wilderness?" he thought, with a down sinking of soul. He
never knew what was coming next, so far as Indian movements were
concerned. Anything might happen.

Now, to his dismay, he heard outside, but apparently quite near,
the howling of a wolf. A hungry wolf, Stephen felt sure. He knew the
sound well, for many a night had he heard wolves howling around
Deerfield's stockade.

The fierce howling drew nearer and nearer.

"He scents me from afar," thought Stephen.

He looked about for some weapon to defend himself, but found
nothing better than his pointed walking staff. This he seized, springing
to his feet, and taking a stand by the wigwam's entrance, thinking:

"I will jab him in the eyes if he comes at me."

The howling ceased. In at the wigwam's opening cam Kewakcum,
laughing in high glee when he found Stephen standing with his stick,

prepared to fight a wolf. This was a great compliment to the natural-ness of his imitation of the wolf's howl.

"Cosannip thought Kewakcum was our brother Shunktokecha, the wolf. Cosannip meant to make a brave fight. Good. Cosannip make mighty brave before many winters," said Kewakcum, laughing.

Stephen laughed too, partly from relief, and partly from joy that Kewakcum had not deserted him.

"Cosannip is all empty," he said, placing his hand on his stomach. "Cosannip very hungry."

"Kewakcum hungry too," said the Indian boy. "Indians must learn to go without food two, three, seven days, sometimes, or they can never be great warriors, go out on the warpath. And they must be up in the morning with the birds. Cosannip lazy, sleep much, like the white man."

"Cosannip very tired, and his foot hurts him," said Stephen.

"Come out in the woods, and see if we can find something to eat," said Kewakcum.

This was a most welcome proposal to Stephen. He had faith in the resources of this lithe, bright-eyed Indian boy, who was so at home in the woods, and of such ready wits. Surely Kewakcum would find something to stay their hunger.

Kewakcum took his bow and arrow, and the two boys set out on their anxious quest, Stephen careful today to keep in sight of his comrade, lest he be again lost.

"Kewakcum kill some chipmunks," said the Indian boy, cheerfully.

"I'm sure you will," said Stephen, believing Kewakcum would do anything he undertook.

Kewakcum made Stephen glide along like himself, without talking, slipping from tree to tree, lest they frighten any possible game. As they walked, Kewakcum's quick, bright eyes were on the alert, scanning the trees on every side. Nothing escaped his notice.

The winter had been unusually severe, and still lingered in these northern woods. Not a chipmunk showed himself. At last, Kewakcum gave up the vain quest, saying:

"Must eat bark."

Looking about, he soon discovered a young black birch. Prying up ends of the bark with his knife, he and Stephen managed to pull off long strips. This was the best that could be done for food, apparently.

"Sun high up above treetops," said Kewakcum, pointing to the sun, nearly overhead. "Go back to wigwam and rest. Then we try the woods again, towards the great river, that way," he added, pointing to the east. "Maybe have better luck."

He led the way back to the wigwam, winding about in the mazes of the forest, yet taking the most direct course for the wigwam with a sure instinct that made Stephen wonder. He was certain he could never have found the wigwam alone.

"How does Kewakcum know his way when there is no road?" he asked.

"Ho, plenty ways," said Kewakcum. "By and by, when Cosannip is bigger Indian, him know the way too, easy enough."

The boys fed their fire with fresh fuel, and then sat down by it and chewed their birch bark. It was not food, it did not satisfy their hunger, but perhaps it aided to sustain life in their desperate strait.

As they sat thus munching bark, suddenly Kewakcum grasped his bow and arrow and sprang to his feet.

"What is it? What do you hear?" asked Stephen alarmed. "Hark! Kewakcum hears footsteps. Someone comes."

Kewakcum peered cautiously out of the wigwam. Then, dropping his weapons, he sprang out, crying joyously:

"Walahowey!"

Stephen too rushed out. He saw a young Indian girl, about Kewakcum's age, approaching, wrapped in a blanket, her head bare. Her thick black hair was parted on top and braided in two heavy braids, hanging down her back.

"Ho, ho, Kewakcum," she said, smiling pleasantly at sight of her cousin, for such he was. Then she stared with lively curiosity at the little pale-faced captive, of whom she had heard, brought all the way from Deerfield to be adopted into her tribe.

"What brings Walahowey?" asked Kewakcum, looking with eager expectation at the hand which the Indian girl held under her blanket.

Walahowey said nothing, but with a smile extended the hidden hand to Kewakcum. Oh, joy! It held several strips of dried moose meat. Was ever sight more welcome than this to the two famished boys?

Stephen thought that never had he tasted anything more delicious. Imitating Kewakcum, he held some of the meat on a pointed stick to toast over the fire. The odor of the burning meat was so appetizing!

But while it cooked, like Kewakcum also, he fell to gnawing away, like a hungry dog, at a raw strip of the meat.

Walahowey watched the boys with pleasure. She herself had known the pangs of keen hunger often enough to be able to sympathize with their satisfaction now.

Presently she told them that her family, who had built these wigwams in which the boys had lodged, were now located farther away, "towards the north star," she said, and that Mummumcott was with them, and had sent her to bid Kewakcum and Stephen join him.

In a very short time the last scrap of the meat, which Kewakcum had scrupulously divided evenly with Stephen, had disappeared. Walahowey then led the way off through the woods north towards Stephen's next home, if "home" be the proper name for his stopping places among the Indians.

The boys started with packs lashed on their backs. Kewakcum had no difficulty in keeping up with the light-footed Indian girl, but Stephen, whose foot hurt badly, limped far behind.

By and by, Walahowey turned, and seeing Stephen limping painfully so far in the rear, went back to him, saying:

"Walahowey carry the pack. Pale-face boy not used to pack. By and by he grow much strong, like the Indian."

So saying, she unbound the burden from Stephen's shoulders, and swinging it deftly over her own, walked on as easily and lightly as if unencumbered.

Stephen now found it much easier to keep up. But his friend Kewakcum looked scowlingly at him, saying:

"Cosannip is good for naught. A squaw is stronger than he."

Stephen felt annoyed, but made no reply, having already begun to learn the Indian lesson of reticence. But Walahowey came to his defense, saying:

"Cosannip's foot is lame and sore. He is new in Indian ways. By and by, when he has lived with the Indians many moons, his heart will be brave and strong, like the Indians."

Stephen felt grateful to Walahowey, but his heart sank within him at her words. Must he, indeed, always live with the Indians, grow up among them, to be, in life and habits, a real Indian, perhaps never again to see a white face? He had heard of white boys and girls captured young, who had grown up among their captors, becoming to all intents genuine Indians.

He could see no hope ahead. Here he was, many miles from any white settlement, alone with the Indians in this wild northern wilderness, with not the faintest prospect of rescue or escape so far as human eye could see.

Stephen's thoughts ran on thus as he plodded along behind his two companions, who maintained the Indians' habitual silence. Plainly there was no earthly hope. But God could see. He could help. And the little boy's heart, in his desolation, rose in silent prayer, that God would do what seemed impossible to men, and yet rescue Stephen from the Indians, perhaps even bring him home again to Deerfield, though that seemed too great happiness to expect.

They tramped on ten miles to the north. Towards night, again Stephen saw the pointed tops of several wigwams rising among the trees ahead. But these wigwams, unlike the others, showed plainly signs of occupation.

Blue smoke curled up from the openings in their tops. Two dogs ran out barking furiously as they saw the children approaching, and a squaw, coming from the forest, bent over under her backload of wood, smiled pleasantly when she saw her nephew, Kewakcum, saying:

"Ho, ho, Kewakcum. Is it well with you?"

"Wurregen *(It is well)*," said Kewakcum. "See, Outenen, I bring you a new nephew, Cosannip."

"Welcome, Cosannip," said Outenen, gazing not unkindly on the little pale-faced boy, who looked so tired and delicate compared with the strong, red-skinned, black-eyed Indian children.

"Little Cosannip come and rest by the fire," said Outenen.

The mother instinct is the same, no matter what the color of the skin, and even in savage women, unless of exceptionally cruel nature, it goes out warmly towards any helpless child.

So Outenen took Stephen into her own wigwam, made him lie down on a bed of skins by the fire, and taking off his moccasins, rubbed softly the sore, tired little feet. She gave him also some more of the moose meat, some of which hung in strips on a leather strap stretched across the wigwam's top, above the fire, drying in the smoke and heat.

The kindness, the motherly touch, somehow melted Stephen's heart with unbearable longings for home and mother. Tears filled his eyes overfull and rolled down his cheeks, in spite of his efforts to repress them.

"The pale-face must not weep," said Outenen. "Only papooses cry. Boys never cry. Now Cosannip's heart is soft because his mind goes back to his father's wigwam. But soon he will love the Indian life best. Then his heart will be strong."

This thought was hardly comforting to Stephen. But at this moment he heard Mummumcott's voice outside, and hurriedly wiped away his tears, fear helping him to self-control.

Mummumcott entered and stood looking at Stephen, giving a grunt of satisfaction that his captive had arrived safely and, on the whole, in such good condition. Saying nothing, he soon left, for all the Indian warriors were to hold a smoke-talk in another wigwam that night to consider future plans. Hunting had been so unsuccessful that some new plan must be devised, as food was again nearly exhausted.

Stephen, in his unusually comfortable state, fell quickly asleep, undisturbed by the chattering of the squaws and children clustered around the fire.

# 15

# MEETING OLD FRIENDS

THE Indian men were off to the hunt the next morning before Stephen woke. He came out of his wigwam, and was standing, wondering if he should have any breakfast, when he saw a squaw running to Outenen, talking excitedly, and pointing to the south.

In a few moments more Stephen saw advancing through the woods what seemed a small army, as in fact it proved to be, for, on closer approach, Stephen recognized the Frenchmen who had made part of the force attacking Deerfield. Having separated from most of their allies, they were taking their own route to Canada. Of their Indian allies, some, as has been said, had started directly for Canada with their captives; some, like Mummumcott and his kin, still lingered in what is now Northern Vermont, always a favorite hunting-ground of the Abenakis, while a few still remained with the French.

As the army marched past, one of these Indians came and spoke to Outenen, who seemed eagerly to assent to some proposal made by him, as Stephen noticed.

This Indian disappeared towards the rear of the army, and soon Stephen saw slowly coming from that direction two men dressed like Indians, but whose faces, in spite of the dirt and smoke darkening them, seemed to be white. They walked feebly, as if in depression of both body and spirit.

As they drew nearer, Stephen, in spite of the sad change in him, recognized, to his delight, his old neighbor, Deacon David Hoyt. Hardly able to believe his eyes, Stephen ran to the deacon, grasping his hand, at first too overpowered by joy and surprise to speak. It was so delightful to see again a white face, and the face, too, of an old friend, part of the dear home life at Deerfield.

Deacon Hoyt, exhausted by fatigue, sorrow, and famine, almost too weak to walk,—indeed, this was the reason his Indian master had left him behind,—looked wonderingly at this little boy in Indian dress of skins, his matted hair hanging over his eyes, his face darkened by smoke, dirt, and tan, not realizing that he had ever seen him.

His companion, Jacob Hix, a Connecticut soldier who had been quartered at Thomas French's, opposite the minister's, and so had often seen Stephen playing about home in the old days, having younger and sharper eyes than the deacon's, exclaimed:

"Why, deacon, don't you see? If I'm not mistaken, it is, —yes, it really is, little Stephen Williams!"

"Stephen, is it possible? Poor child! Can it be that my minister's son has come to this?" cried Deacon Hoyt, gazing on the neglected-looking child before him with surprise and sorrow.

"Oh, I am so glad to see you and Jacob," said Stephen. "I thought perhaps I should never see English people any more. And now to see two old friends from Deerfield seems too good to be true, almost."

"Ah, poor boy, I fear it is but sorry fortune that brings us three from Deerfield together here in the wilderness," said the deacon. "But if our coming cheers you, I am glad."

"Have you seen my father?" asked Stephen eagerly, looking after the Frenchmen disappearing over a hill in the distance as if he would run to join them were his father there, so near. "Were any of my brothers and sisters in your company?"

"No," said the deacon. "Jacob and I were the only captives in this company. The rest are scattered about with their Indian masters, no one knows where. I need not ask if food has been plentiful with you, Stephen. Your thin, pinched face and body show that you have suffered as we have."

"The deacon and I are near the last point from starvation," said Hix.

"I feel that I cannot hold out much longer," said the deacon. "The Lord's will be done! I thank God I can still say that, even though I cannot understand why such terrible sufferings are permitted to fall upon God's people. But soon I shall know. I am ready to depart and be at rest."

In truth, the deacon's heart and spirit were broken. More prostrating even than the physical suffering he had endured had been his heart-breaking anguish in seeing his home destroyed and his whole family carried off into captivity, except the oldest daughter, Mary, who, fortunately for her, had been away from home on a visit to Hatfield the day of the attack, and his son Benjamin, a lad of thirteen, who had escaped capture by hiding in a bin of grain. His oldest son and namesake had been killed in the meadow fight. Hardest of all, his two youngest children, his peculiar pets, as the youngest in a family often are, Abigail, a baby of two, and Ebenezer, a boy of eight, he had seen slain by the Indians during this terrible journey. His loved wife, his son Jonathan, and beautiful daughter Sarah were captives somewhere among the Indians, he knew not where, or what they might be enduring if still alive. It is little wonder that a life suddenly stripped so bare had ceased to hold him strongly.

Both he and Hix showed but too plainly what they had suffered. The deacon, although a man of only fifty-two years, was shrunken, wasted and wrinkled until he seemed rather to be in the seventies,—an infirm, tottering old man.

Jacob, a stalwart young man in the prime of life, was wasted to skin and bone, and also walked with difficulty.

Stephen, full of pity for his friends, and anxious to help them, said:

"I will run and ask Outenen for some dried moose meat for you. It is delicious."

"Anything in the shape of food would taste good to us now, I guess," said Jacob.

Outenen had been pleased with the chance to acquire two more captives. Therefore, when Stephen timidly asked food of her for his friends, she willingly gave him a few small pieces of meat, besides a bit for his own breakfast, though saying:

"Indians have bad luck lately. Great Spirit angry, no smile on the hunt. Before many suns Indians starve unless Great Spirit is appeased."

Even this small portion of food which Stephen brought his friends was a great boon to them. As he watched them devouring it, he said:

"How I hope we can all stay together now! I don't feel so lonely with you both here. I feel as if you would take care of me."

"Unluckily it is little we can do for you, no matter how good our will," said Jacob.

"No, we are all helpless captives in the hands of cruel savages. I had to stand helplessly by and see my own little ones slain," said Deacon Hoyt, sadly. "We can only pity you."

"Even that helps a little, to know that some one cares, some one is sorry," said Stephen. "The Indians don't care, no matter what happens to me."

Later in the day Kewakcum called Stephen, saying:

"Cosannip, come. Kewakcum make him a bow and arrow like his."

Stephen was pleased at this, and sat watching Kewakcum with great interest, to see exactly how the Indians made their weapons. Kewakcum brought from his wigwam a piece of seasoned ash wood, from which he cut a strip for the bow. He scraped it hard, and rubbed it down with sand, till it was smooth and shining. Then he rubbed into it a little of the precious bear's grease from Outenen's slender store which hung from her wigwam pole in a skin bag. This added to its suppleness.

"Ho, it bends well," said Kewakcum, as he bent and tested the stick thus prepared.

Next he cut notches in each end, to which he tied a strong bowstring made from the sinews of a deer. Stephen took the bow with great satisfaction when done, wishing he could show it to some of the Deerfield boys, while Kewakcum proceeded to make three arrows. For these he used reeds whose stalks were like bamboo,—hollow, straight and light.

Splitting one end of each, he tied in securely with sinews a head made of a sharp-pointed flint. He had a number of these flints in a pouch gayly embroidered with beads, which hung at his belt. To the arrow's other end he tied a few birds' feathers, which he also took from his pouch, which was evidently the storehouse of all his boyish wealth.

On each arrow, Kewakcum cut a little crooked mark, saying to Stephen:

"That Cosannip's mark. Know his arrow wherever it flies."

Walahowey, who had also been watching the work, now brought Stephen a long, narrow pouch or bag of skin, embroidered with beads; a quiver to carry his arrows, like those used by the Indians.

"Walahowey sew that herself," she said proudly.

"Thank you, Walahowey, I like it very much," said Stephen, happy in these new possessions.

"Now come," said Kewakcum. "Kewakcum teach Cosannip to hunt, same as Indians."

The white boy and the red tramped off into the woods together, carrying their bows, their arrows in the quivers slung on their backs. Kewakcum instructed Stephen that it was important never to lose an arrow. In shooting small animals he must try to aim at them when on or near a tree trunk, so that, if the arrow missed, it would either stick fast in the tree or rebound back towards him. If shot off at random into the tree branches, it might go far on into the woods and be lost.

The sun shone brightly and the day seemed hopeful and springlike. Could Stephen only have had enough food to still his constant gnawing sense of hunger, he would have been almost happy as he trudged along behind Kewakcum, watching the trees intently for birds or squirrels.

"How good some roast squirrel meat would taste," thought Stephen. "I do hope we shall shoot some squirrels. I guess Kewakcum will find them if any one can."

After a while Kewakcum stopped, directing Stephen's attention to some round holes in the snow near the foot of a tree.

"Good," he said. "Bright sun bring chipmunk out. Him think spring come. Now Indian boys have much sport."

Kewakcum now proceeded more cautiously than before. Soon he hid behind a tree trunk, motioning Stephen to do the same, and pointing to a large oak, a giant of the forest, on or around which Kewakcum's keen eyes had detected some signs of the desired game which Stephen could not see. But he obeyed orders, and hid behind another tree trunk near Kewakcum.

The boys, peeping stealthily around their trees, were soon gladdened by seeing two fine chipmunks sportively chasing each other up the oak's huge trunk. Straight from Kewakcum's bow sped an arrow, bringing one of the pretty creatures tumbling to the ground.

Stephen, almost trembling with eager excitement, shot also. But his chipmunk skipped nimbly away up into the tree branches, running with a lightning-like rapidity. Kewakcum sent another arrow flying after it, but the chipmunk, winged by terror, dashed out on the extreme end of a topmost bough, and, giving a flying leap, landed in the top of a thick pine, where it concealed itself, and was safe.

"Brave boy, that chipmunk. Save his skin that time," said Kewakcum, as he picked up his own game.

"I don't see why my arrow didn't hit him," said Stephen. "I aimed right at him, but when my arrow got there he wasn't there! I hit the tree, anyway," he said, as he picked up his arrow, rather crestfallen at his ill luck.

"Cosannip must practice, so he can hit the bird on the wing," said Kewakcum. "Indian boys always practice. Begin when little papoose."

The boys hunted a while longer, but chipmunks were not yet plentiful, and they found no other game. So they returned to camp, and Kewakcum proceeded to cook his chipmunk.

He dug a hole into the ashes under the fire's hot coals, and to Stephen's surprise thrust in the chipmunk just as it was, without removing the skin, covering it with hot ashes, then with coals.

When Kewakcum thought the game done he drew it forth, stripping off the skin, which now peeled off easily. Stephen, meantime, had stood watching the cooking with hungry eyes, wondering if he should have a taste of the feast.

Kewakcum was generous. He shared his roast chipmunk with all the children, Walahowey and Stephen each having a hind leg for their portion. It was a small morsel, but aggravatingly delicious to the hungry Stephen, who sucked the tiny bone dry and bare, and then did not disdain to share with Kewakcum the half of the skin which Kewakcum gave him, gnawing at it inside with as keen relish as the Indian boy.

"I wish Deacon Hoyt and Jacob could have had a taste of that chipmunk," thought Stephen. "But perhaps it would only make them more hungry, as it does me; it was so good and so small."

Here Kewakcum called, "Come, Cosannip. Come learn to shoot like Indian."

Stephen was anxious to do this, so he gladly followed Kewakcum into an open meadow across the brook from the camp. He supposed that Kewakcum would set him to firing at a mark. But not at all. On the contrary, Kewakcum began throwing snowballs and sticks up into the air, expecting Stephen to shoot and hit them before they reached the ground.

"Of course I can never hit such things as that," said Stephen disgusted. "No one could. Put a mark up on the tree trunk, and let me aim at that."

"Ho, ho," cried Kewakcum, contemptuously, "a papoose two winters old could do that! If Cosannip want to be true Indian—"

"I don't," thought Stephen, but careful not to think aloud.

"He must learn to shoot things in motion," continued Kewakcum. "Do the deer and the moose stand still in the forest, or the wild bird and squirrel sit down on a branch, waiting for the hunter to shoot them? No, no. Every creature runs, flies, darts swiftly away, to save its skin. Indian must be spryer than the creatures."

This seemed impossible to Stephen. But he found he must at least try, so he did his best to hit the objects Kewakcum kept tossing up. He hit nothing, however, save once, unluckily, the top of Kewakcum's head, the arrow grazing through the thick hair uncomfortably near the scalp.

"Ho, ho," cried Kewakcum, laughing good-naturedly, to Stephen's relief, who feared he would be angry. "Cosannip kill Kewakcum next thing, him no look out sharp."

"I'm sorry, Kewakcum. I didn't mean to," said Stephen, as he ran to pick up his arrow.

But even if he had hit nothing, he found that he was gradually getting better command of his bow, feeling more sure, more at home with it.

Not averse to displaying his skill, Kewakcum now had Stephen toss up snowballs for him to aim at, hitting the flying balls more than once, to Stephen's unbounded admiration. When towards sunset they returned to camp, Kewakcum, in the best of spirits, said:

"Tomorrow, before the sun up, Kewakcum, he bark like fox outside Mummumcott's wigwam for Cosannip to come out. Go hunt the chipmunk in the dawn. Good time then. Kewakcum knows a charm that will bring the chipmunks around him thick as flies. Bring home big load of chipmunks, maybe."

Stephen was glad to find that Deacon Hoyt was assigned that night to the same wigwam where he slept. It seemed almost like being near his father to curl up beside this familiar friend from Deerfield, father of some of his former playmates. And the deacon's heart warmed towards this homeless child, son of his minister, in such forlorn surroundings.

He knew not where his own children slept that night. But it comforted him to say kindly to Stephen, ere they fell asleep:

"I trust, my child, though thus alone among the heathen, you do not forget your pious father's teachings."

No, Deacon Hoyt. I pray to God, asking Him to take care of me, every night before I fall asleep, and every morning too, in my heart."

"That is right. It would gladden your father's sorrowful heart could he know that. We must cling to our religious faith. Only that is left us now."

# 16

# AFTER A FAST, A FEAST

KEWAKCUM'S fine plan for an early morning chipmunk hunt was not destined to succeed. Mummumcott and his companions returned from the hunt that night in apparent good spirits, even though bringing in no game. But they ordered the camp be broken up forthwith, for some reason unknown to the captives. They always felt a vague alarm at any change, because it was likely to bring them worse conditions, rather than better.

In the early dawn next morning Outenen and the other squaws fell busily to work, stripping the skins from the beds of boughs and the wigwams, and doing their cooking utensils and few other possessions up in long rolls tied in the skins, each shouldering as heavy a pack as she could well walk under. Deacon Hoyt and Jacob, being captives, were laden with packs, even in their weak condition, and Stephen also was required to bear a small one.

Kewakcum stalked off unburdened, like the braves, who, now that their squaws were with them, calmly left all drudgery to them and the captives.

Stephen felt this so strange that he ventured to ask Kewakcum:

"Why don't the men help? They are much bigger and stronger than the squaws. Englishmen never let their wives carry loads. They carry them themselves. They think it the man's part, because he is stronger."

"Ho, Englishmen fools; part squaw themselves; no warriors," was Kewakcum's scornful reply. "Warriors must not work. They must keep their hearts strong, to go on the hunt and the warpath. Work is for squaws and Englishmen."

Stephen made no reply. His point of view was so different from Kewakcum's that he saw argument to be useless.

They had walked some miles when Kewakcum came to Stephen with this information.

"Good news. Mummumcott and the other hunters had good luck. Plenty feast pretty soon. Plenty for all."

This was indeed the best of news, and Stephen cheered the hearts of the deacon and Jacob by telling it to them at the first opportunity. All marched on more easily, for hope buoys up body as well as spirit. They had eaten nothing that day, the supply of dried moose meat being wholly exhausted, and the hope of an abundance of food soon was indeed reviving.

After walking eight miles or more they came to an opening in the woods, on a hillside sloping to the south, near a brook. Here, in the edge of the wood was the welcome spectacle of two great moose hanging, which the hunters had by great good fortune slain the previous day. They had now moved their camp up to the moose, and would stay there until the meat was eaten or dried for future use.

As soon as they had erected the wigwams the squaws went to work dressing the moose, skinning the bodies with a deftness taught by long practice. Outenen was the fortunate possessor of an iron knife, made from a piece of hoop iron, sharpened and set in a wooden handle, and with this she made quick work.

While thus engaged, Outenen directed Kewakcum to build a big fire for the coming feast on the ground in the centre of the space around which stood the wigwams. The squaws had cleared away all snow from this spot.

"Go, Cosannip, bring wood for the fire," commanded Outenen.

Stephen and Kewakcum went out into the surrounding woods. Wood was plentiful here, dead branches and limbs of fallen trees everywhere strewing the ground. Kewakcum managed to hew off some quite large branches with a small axe he had been allowed to take, a much prized trophy brought by Mummumcott from Deerfield.

Before long the boys returned, Stephen bending over under his load of branches whose ends trailed on the ground behind him. Kewakcum walked behind him swinging the axe in an easy, masterful way, unburdened, save as he carried an armful of dead wood and light stuff he had gathered for kindling.

"Do but look at poor little Stephen," whispered Jacob to the deacon. "It galls me to see Minister Williams's son a bound slave to these savages."

"How long, O Lord, how long, wilt Thou suffer the heathen to flourish?" groaned the deacon.

When Stephen was relieved of his load he sat down, exhausted, on the ground, watching Kewakcum. He wondered how Kewakcum would manage to start a fire without flint or tinder. But Kewakcum set confidently to work. First he made a tiny pile of light, dry stuff, easily kindled. Then he took from one of the packs two fire-sticks made of cedar wood. One served as the hearth. It was flat, with four round holes in it. A little notch was cut on one side of each cavity to allow the air to get at the heated wood dust, and also that the dust, when afire, might be quickly thrust into the pile of kindling close by. The fire-sticks were always kept as dry as possible. The end of the upper stick exactly fitted the hollows in the hearth, which were blackened by smoke and fire from former use. Placing the end of the upper stick in one of the hollows, Kewakcum attached his bow-string around it. Then, pushing the bow back and forth swiftly, the upper stick revolved with great rapidity in the hollow of the lower one.

By and by, after patient work, sparks began to fly, which Kewakcum deftly caught on his dry stuff, igniting it. Over this tiny blaze he erected a little tent the size of a teacup, made of dry pine sticks. When this, too, blazed, he gradually added more kindling, until at last he was able to throw on great logs, and the fire burned high under the sky.

"Well done, boy," Jacob Hix could not help saying.

"Isn't Kewakcum smart? He can do anything," said Stephen, filled with admiration at his Indian friend's success.

"Certainly he has done well this time," said Deacon Hoyt, his spirits cheered by the bright fire and the prospect of food.

Kewakcum was much pleased with these compliments to his skill. But he was careful to maintain a stolid face, not deigning to show his pleasure. An Indian boy early learns that it is weak, womanish, to show emotion. Whatever happens, of joy or misfortune, he must be superior to it; receive it stoically.

A trophy brought from Deerfield which the Indians greatly valued was a big brass kettle taken from the Williams house. The squaws, driving poles with crotched ends down into the ground each side the fire, placed another stick across the crotches to support this kettle. The ice in the stream was softening in the March sunshine. They broke it by jabbing it with instruments which they carried for this purpose made of sharp-pointed deer and moose horns fastened into long wooden handles. This done, they ordered Hoyt and Jacob to fill the kettle with water and bring it up the hill.

"To think I should live to be under petticoat government," groaned Jacob to himself. "And no petticoats at that," he added, glancing at the squaws' fringed buckskin leggings and skin coats, barely reaching their knees. "I'm glad none of my fellow-soldiers are here to see me. Though doubtless they would have to serve, too, if here. And to think of Deacon Hoyt coming to this!"

Well did he remember the deacon, sitting on high in the deacons' seat in the Deerfield meeting-house, the picture of decent self-respect, gazing down on the congregation with serene dignity. And now to see him, dirty, hair uncombed, beard unshorn, clad in squalid Indian garments, feeble and suffering, a slave, compelled to do the bidding of Indian squaws!

Stephen sat gazing ruefully at the brass kettle which the squaws had hung over the fire and were filling with chunks of moose meat. Pangs of homesickness rent his heart. How often had he seen that kettle, gleaming brightly, swinging from the crane in the big fireplace at home, while savory odors filled the cheerful living-room; Parthena stepping briskly about; his mother, baby in arms, with tender smile and loving words calling her children to the table, where sat his father, serene and happy in his dear home,' all his loved ones around him! And now, where were they all? Perhaps all cruelly killed, like his dear mother and her little ones. Probably he should never see them again.

As these sad thoughts filled his mind, in spite of himself Stephen's eyes overflowed with the tears that drowned them. He tried hurriedly to wipe them away, but Kewakcum's quick eyes spied them. He said in haughty tone:

''Ho, Cosannip a squaw. No warrior. Never go out on the warpath, and come home rich in scalps and captives, like other Indians. Stay in camp, dig, plant, hoe, with the squaws.''

And Kewakcum went off in disgust.

Jacob Hix saw Stephen's trouble, and when chance offered said to him:

''Cheer up, Stephen. That moose meat cooking smells wondrous appetizing. At least we shall have our fill of food for once, unless I am woefully mistaken.''

"Maybe they will not give us captives any," said Stephen, dolefully.

The boy was really worn out with hardship and hunger, and felt utterly hopeless.

The moment the meat was cooked the squaws dipped out large bowls full of the hot stew and presented them to their lords and masters, who, thrusting their hands into the bowls, helped themselves to great mouthfuls of the meat, swallowing it almost whole, making way with bowlful after bowlful. When at last they could hold no more, they wiped their hands on their hair, or the back of some dog sniffing hungrily around, and then, taking the pipes filled and lighted by their squaws, lay back in the ease of perfect satiety.

Now the squaws and children might presume to eat. And now, too, came the happy moment when to each starving captive was given a big bowlful of the hot stew. There was no salt, no seasoning of any sort, no bread or vegetables to eat with it; but hunger was an all-sufficient relish, and the captives had hardly since they left home made so satisfying a meal.

Kewakcum, who seemed to have forgotten his momentary difference with Stephen, came bringing him a piece of meat in his fingers.

"Eat," he said. "Mummumcott gave it to Kewakcum. Kewakcum he give taste to Cosannip."

"What is it?" asked Stephen.

"Piece of moose's fat nose. Heap sweet meat. Best part," said Kewakcum.

Kewakcum's hands were far from clean, and once moose's nose would not have sounded inviting to Stephen. But he did not like to offend Kewakcum by refusing what was meant for a great kindness, nor was he in a condition to be over particular. So he accepted the gift, and found the morsel sweet and tender, as Kewakcum had said.

He felt sorry for the dogs, who were hanging hungrily around, getting only kicks if they became too obtrusive. He knew so well what hunger was that he could not help sympathizing with the dogs. When the dog he liked best, whom he had privately named Spot, came whining and begging around him, Stephen, hungry as he was, spared a bone with some meat still on it, for his dog friend. Spot eagerly seized it and was making off with his treasure when, to Stephen's surprise, Kewakcum snatched away the bone and threw it into the fire, saying:

"Bad. Very bad. Never give moose's bones to a dog. Moose spirit see it, be very angry. Moose come no more."

"But what will the poor dogs do? They will starve," said Stephen.

"By and by, when moose spirit not looking, squaws will give the dogs some meat. But the moose will know it, and be very angry, if dogs gnaw his bones."

Later Stephen learned the superstitious reverence felt by the Indians for the bones of any creature. Bones of animals were either burned or buried, lest the animal's spirit be offended. To give an animal's bones to a dog was believed to be especially offensive to the animal's spirit, and sure to bring ill luck in hunting. If removing permanently to a distance, the Indians always, if possible, took with them the bones of their own dead. If an Indian were slain in battle, his friends made desperate efforts to recover his body and give it burial. The spirit was supposed to be still, in some mysterious way, connected with its former abode, and aware of either neglect or tender care in its treatment.

After all had eaten, Stephen saw Outenen, with what seemed a respectful address to the spirit of the moose, calculated to appease his injured feelings, give the poor dogs a full meal also, after which they lay around the fire in a state of dog happiness and satisfaction beautiful to behold. Peace and content brooded over the whole camp that night, even the captives enjoying a sweet, restful sleep.

The next day, while the Indian men lay around the camp, not exerting themselves to hunt while food was so plentiful, the squaws worked hard caring for a portion of the meat, cutting it into long strips and hanging it up to dry; a part on frames in the sunshine, a part on lines stretched across the interior of the wigwams, above the fires. The skins were also carefully prepared and put drying.

The prodigality of the Indians, in thus lying about and gorging themselves in lazy ease while food was abundant, amazed the thrifty Deerfield deacon, and he said to Hix:

"It passes my understanding how these savages can be such short-sighted spendthrifts. At this rate, their meat will soon be gone, and they may not have another such stroke of luck for many days. Think how long we have been starving. Soon they will come to pinching again."

"I ventured to say as much to one of them," said Hix. "I said, 'Better not stuff so much now. By and by Indians starve again.' He said, 'Ho, Indian no care. Indian he go seven, eight days without eating, easy enough. Indian wise. He fill himself full when the Good Spirit send plenty.'"

Mummumcott had left his family in Northern Vermont when he had joined the war party going down against Deerfield. As yet he had not found them, though knowing them to be somewhere in this tract of country. After one more day spent in feasting, he set off in search of his family, taking his nephew, Kewakcum, with him, but to Stephen's surprise and joy, leaving him behind. Stephen said to Jacob:

"I am so glad that Mummumcott did not take me away, because I love to be with you and Deacon Hoyt. I am thankful to Mummumcott for once, no matter what comes. It is such a comfort to be with English people and old Deerfield friends."

"I hope the Indians will leave us together after this," said Jacob. "True, we are all helpless alike in their hands, and it is little we can do for one another. But misery loves company. And we will help you if we can, Stephen, you may depend on that."

"I know it, and it seems so good to be with some one who cares," said Stephen. "It is almost too good to be true that Mummumcott has really left me with you."

So, alas, it proved, for only two mornings later a strange Indian stalked out of the forest into the camp. The other Indians seemed to know him, and proceeded at once to feast the guest, as Indian etiquette demanded. When he had eaten all he could, Outenen came to the place where Stephen was sitting, playing with Spot, who often hung about him, seeming conscious of the warm place for him in the boy's heart, saying:

"Cosannip make ready to go to Mummumcott. He find his family. He send Teokunhko the Swift to bring Cosannip to his wigwam."

"But I don't want to go. I would rather stay here with my old friends, Deacon Hoyt and Jacob," cried Stephen in dismay, his face full of distress.

"Must go. Mummumcott has said so. Cosannip is Mummumcott's captive," was Outenen's only reply.

Teokunhko, a tall, straight, lithe young brave, had slung his quiver over his back, and stood, bow in hand, his face cold and stern, impatient to be off.

"O Deacon Hoyt, Jacob," cried Stephen, running to his friends, tears streaming down his cheeks. "Do you hear? I've got to go away from you, off by myself, alone with the Indians again. Oh, I don't want to go!"

"Poor, poor child," said the deacon, sympathy for Stephen making him hardly able to speak.

"It's too bad, Stephen, my boy," said Jacob, "but I suppose there is no help for it. To resist will only anger the Indians, and get you into fresh trouble. Remember the old saying, 'While there is life there is hope.' We must try to keep up our courage to the last, and keep on hoping, dark as everything looks now."

"My child," said the deacon, "I fear there is no help for you. We must say good-by, probably to meet no more in this world of sorrow. Remember my last words, Stephen. Whatever happens, cling fast to your trust in God."

Teokunhko, who had looked on with visibly increasing impatience, at this point took hold of Stephen's shoulder, and set off with him.

"Good-by, Deacon. Good-by, Jacob," cried Stephen, turning his sorrowful face, down whose stained cheeks the tears had washed little courses, back over his shoulder for a last look at his friends, as Teokunhko relentlessly dragged him away. Then Teokunhko and his little charge disappeared in the shades of the forest, and Stephen's friends saw him no more. Something that had lent a degree of pleasure to their forlorn lives passed out of them with the going away of the little boy.

# 17

# A TEDIOUS DAY'S TRAVEL

TEOKUNHKO had not been idly named "the swift one." With soft, silent tread and long stride, he sped on, up hill and down dale, through forest, over brooks, across swamps, and through bushy, thorny undergrowth, over mossy, fallen logs, down the sides of rocky ravines, as sure-footed as a mountain goat, at a pace hard for poor, lame, down-hearted little Stephen to maintain. He did his very best to follow closely, for this strange Indian looked stern and hard, and Stephen, alone with him in the woods, believed that, should he falter, Teokunhko would think no more of killing him than had he been a rabbit or chipmunk.

Luckily he was supported by a good breakfast that morning of warm moose meat, which gave him greater strength. Spurred on by fear, he kept up fairly well at first. But a long day's travel was necessary, even at the pace maintained by Teokunhko, to reach Mummumcott's wigwam. By the time the sun began to sink a little toward the west, Stephen felt his strength waning sadly, and his foot grew lamer and lamer. He struggled on for a while. At last in utter despair he cast himself, panting, on the ground, unable to take another step, and awaited the worst, crying in his heart:

"Our Father who art in heaven, please help me now!" Teokunhko, far in advance, out of sight among a thick cluster of low-growing evergreens, suddenly turned and discovered that his charge was not in sight. He came striding swiftly back.

"Now he will surely kill me," thought Stephen, looking up piteously into the stern, dark face, but not daring to cry or entreat.

Teokunhko gave a grunt of disgust when he saw the helpless condition of the boy. He seized him roughly, but instead of dashing out his brains then and there, as the trembling Stephen expected, he tossed the boy over his shoulder, settled his burden firmly on his back, took a leg of Stephen under each arm, and, though thus laden, sped on more swiftly than before. Whatever Teokunhko might have done had the boy been his own, the captive belonged to Mummumcott, and he was responsible to that warrior for the safe delivery of his property.

So weak was Stephen he could have cried for joy at this sudden deliverance, both from his fears and his toils. But crying would never answer, as he well knew. So he put his arms around Teokunhko's neck, and held tightly on, his heart full of thankfulness.

And now one pleasant thought came to him:

"Perhaps Kewakcum will be there. Oh, I hope he will!"

Kewakcum had seemed to like the little white boy, and had, in a way, made a comrade of him and been kind to him. In his desolation, Stephen's heart reached out eagerly for even the slightest hint of kindness or friendship, as a morning-glory growing in the shade stretches towards a lay of sunlight.

Night descended on the silent forest. Then Stephen heard the solemn "whoo, whoo" of owls, and the howling of wolves in the distance. He clung more tightly to Teokunhko, wondering whether he meant to sleep in the woods, or whether he would travel all night.

Teokunhko gave no hint of his plans, but sped on through the dark as if he had eyes in his feet, in the same grim silence he had observed all day. He knew but few words of English, and it was not the Indian custom to waste words when travelling.

Stephen began to grow so sleepy and tired that he felt in danger of dropping fast asleep and losing his hold, in spite of his desperate effort to keep his heavy eyes open. But suddenly he saw something that made those sleepy eyes open wide,—a glimmer of light through the trees far ahead!

Was it really a light, or had it been only a delusion of his weariness? It had disappeared, for Teokunhko had gone down into a ravine. But as he ascended the other side of the hollow the light again shone out nearer and brighter. Presently Stephen was able to discern that it was the blaze of a fire, and then he saw plainly by its glimmering light the pointed tops of three wigwams.

The end of their long day's journey was at last reached. Teokunhko, apparently as fresh as when he started in the morning, strode up to Mummumcott, who sat by the fire, and slipping Stephen from his back placed him on his feet, though Stephen could hardly stand, saying in Indian tongue:

"Behold the captive. Teokunhko has brought him."

"Wurregen *(It is well),*" said Mummumcott.

He said nothing to Stephen, save to give a grunt of disgust as he saw the boy's feeble condition. Stephen stood forlornly in the firelight, wondering what would become of him, when a joyous voice called:

"Ho, ho, netop *(friend).*"

Turning, there was Kewakcum, smiling, glad to greet again his white playmate.

"O Kewakcum," said Stephen, "I am so glad to see you. Kewakcum," he added with earnest emphasis, "Cosannip very hungry. He has eaten nothing since morning, and he cannot walk."

Kewakcum's quick eyes saw that Stephen was in sorry plight. But, saying nothing, to Stephen's surprise he turned and ran quickly away.

"What shall I do? What will become of me?" thought Stephen. "Even Kewakcum will not help me."

He looked pitifully at Mummumcott's stern face, but saw that little comfort was to be expected from that quarter. Indeed, Mummumcott was beginning to think his white captive a useless burden, and was querying in his own mind whether it would not be wiser to slay him at once, and so rid himself of this encumbrance before he set off next day with his family, as he planned, for a more distant hunting spot, farther towards the Canadian boundary. Evidently the boy was too weak to travel, and would soon die anyway if exposed to further hardships.

As Stephen sat on the ground by the fire, in mute despair and wretchedness, he saw Kewakcum coming from the farthest wigwam with a squaw, to whom he was talking eagerly, pointing towards Stephen. This squaw was Kewakcum's mother, Heelahdee, the wife of Mummumcott's brother, Waneton.

Heelahdee's heavy black hair was parted on her forehead and hung in two long plaits down her back. The parting was stained red with vermilion. Her face, dark red though it was, had a certain charm of its own. Her quick black eyes indicated mental brightness, and she had a pleasant, kindly expression. As Stephen anxiously scanned the face of this newcomer, he was reassured. Evidently Kewakcum, instead of deserting him as he supposed, had brought powerful reinforcements to the rescue.

"Ah, the poor little birdling has fallen out of the nest," said Heelahdee in soft tones, looking with pity on the helpless child. "Come, Cosannip, Heelahdee will brood him under her wings."

"Have no fear, Cosannip," said Kewakcum. "My mother will care for you. She has promised me."

Heelahdee stooped, and easily lifting Stephen, carried him tenderly in her arms to her own wigwam. She spread a soft deerskin, the furry side up, on the bed of pine and hemlock branches, and laid Stephen on it by the fire, covering him with a soft, warm bear skin. Then she brought him a bowlful of stewed bear's meat. After satisfying his craving hunger, Stephen would have fallen instantly to sleep in his comparative comfort but for his frozen toe, which pained him severely.

Kewakcum, who had stood by watching Stephen eat, saw him grasp his foot with an expression of pain, and called his mother's attention to the matter. Heelahdee drew off Stephen's worn moccasin, and examined the foot.

"Ah, poor birdling," she said, with soft murmurs of pity, as she saw the swollen little foot that had travelled so many weary miles since last it trod Deerfield's street.

Heelahdee rubbed the lame foot gently and soothingly with melted bear's fat. Then she did it up carefully in a strip of greased cloth, precious cloth, of which she had only a little, bought the last summer in Montreal in exchange for beaver skins.

Soothed, comfortable, and comforted, Stephen on his warm, soft couch fell fast asleep even while Heelahdee's hands were fastening on the bandage, his last conscious thought being a sleepy effort to pray. The words faltered and failed on his lips, but One who reads the human heart knew the thankfulness filling Stephen's that night.

Kewakcum was a bright boy, the oldest son of Waneton and Heelahdee, regarded by them as giving promise of being some day a great warrior and chief among the Abenakis. He resembled some older sons of white families in that he was a trifle spoiled and apt to get his own way.

So when Kewakcum beset his father that night, after Stephen was asleep, to buy the white captive from Mummumcott, it did not take him long to convince Waneton of the wisdom of his plan.

"Kewakcum wants a brother to go with him to the hunt," he pleaded with bright, eager eyes. "Kewakcum teach his brother to hunt, fish, swim; make heap big brave of Cosannip before many winters. Kewakcum and Cosannip go forth on the warpath like twin bears. The English will tremble in his wigwam when he hears their fierce roar."

Waneton looked with pleased eyes on the animated countenance of his brave, ambitious son. But he only grunted and said:

"Pale-face weakling. No good."

Then up spoke Heelahdee on her boy's side.

"Waneton knows that Kewakcum has no brother of his own age. The papoose is too little to play with and help Kewakcum. Heelahdee will cure the pale-face and make him strong. Before many snows Waneton will have two brave sons to hunt for him and to go on the warpath when Waneton sits in the council of the elders."

"Waneton no give Mummumcott good beaver skins for sick pale-face boy. No good that," said Waneton.

"Trade the dog Anum for him," said Kewakcum. "Mummumcott said today that he needed another dog for the hunt."

Waneton gave a grunt of assent to this proposal, for he was rich in dogs. He sought out Mummumcott and sat down in his wigwam, where, after smoking a pipe together in silence, Waneton finally offered Mummumcott the dog Anum in exchange for his captive.

Mummumcott was secretly pleased with this offer in exchange for property worse than useless to him. "Better a live dog than a dead boy," would have been the language of his heart; but he affected indifference, and held off in seeming reluctance, until at last Waneton was obliged to add a small beaver skin to the price offered for Stephen. This offer was accepted, and Stephen became the property of Waneton.

It was very late when Stephen woke the next morning. When he opened his eyes he found Kewakcum standing beside him.

"Ho, ho, Cosannip," said Kewakcum. "Big news. Let Cosannip's heart sing for joy. Mummumcott gone far away towards the Great Bear," he added, pointing north. "Cosannip he live now in the wigwam of Waneton, be same as brother to Kewakcum. Kewakcum teach Cosannip to hunt, fish, go on warpath before many winters."

Stephen could not but be pleased at this change of fortunes. If he must live among the Indians it was certainly better to be with those who seemed disposed to treat him kindly, so he said:

"Cosannip's heart very glad, Kewakcum."

Then he tried to rise, though so weak and exhausted he felt unable to stir.

But Heelahdee, who had come in, said:

"Cosannip lie still and rest. Heelahdee bring him some broth and some medicine, cure his foot, make him well and strong. Then Cosannip get up and go forth to the hunt with Kewakcum."

Stephen was only too thankful to lie still on his soft, warm bed. It was the first real comfort and rest of body and mind he had known since leaving Deerfield.

He slept and drowsed all day, only half conscious at times of a bright-eyed little Indian girl who sometimes stood beside him, staring at that object of much wonder and interest to her, the pale-faced boy, and hearing but faintly the cooing and cries that came now and then from Heelahdee's papoose, which, strapped in an Indian cradle of bark, was suspended from a pole in the wigwam while its mother was at work outside.

# 18

# THE BOYS HUNT

THE northern woods in the section now comprised in the States of Vermont and New Hampshire had long been a favorite hunting-ground of the Abenaki Indians. The original home of the Abenakis was in northern Maine and southern Canada, but many of them, having become partly Christianized and civilized under the influence of the Jesuit priests, had settled in Canada, near Fort Francis, on the St. Lawrence.

Here they lived during the summer, in a state of semi-civilization. But when the winter hunting season came around the Indians broke up their homes, and taking squaws, children, dogs, and all their possessions set off for the old hunting-grounds, there to return to the life of primitive savagery.

Waneton and his brother Mummumcott has thus far stubbornly resisted all efforts of the Jesuits for their conversion. Heelahdee was a believer, though she dared not give much expression to her faith before Waneton. But she tried as opportunity offered to teach her children to bless themselves, and to pray to the Virgin and to the Saviour.

When Heelahdee ventured to commend the new faith to Waneton, he said sturdily:

"Waneton knows the Great Spirit and the Four Winds. The Great Spirit helps Waneton on the hunt, and the West Wind makes Waneton's heart strong and gives him victory when he goes forth on the warpath against his enemies. Waneton knows not the Frenchman's God. The Great Spirit, the Indian Manitou, will be very angry if Waneton does as the Black Robes bid him; help Waneton no more."

So the Waneton household was divided on religious questions.

It was several days before Stephen regained his strength. Meantime, April, "the Goose Moon," as the Indians called it, had come, though Stephen had no means of knowing either the days of the week or month. But, as one bright morning he stood outside the wigwam in the warm sunshine, he realized that spring was coming fast. He was listening with delight to the first robin he had heard, pouring out the gladness swelling its little heart in a rippling flood of sweetest song, as it lightly poised on the topmost branch of a pine near Stephen.

"Cheer up, cheer up," warbled the little red breast, and Stephen could not help feeling in better heart and hope as he listened.

Suddenly an arrow whizzed close past Stephen, and away flew the robin.

"Bad luck that time," Stephen heard a voice saying behind him.

Turning, he saw Kewakcum and his kinsman, Nunganey, a boy about Stephen's age. The boys had come up so softly that Stephen had not heard them. It was Nunganey who had shot at the robin, and now ran to pick up his arrow, while Kewakcum said:

"Cosannip well now. Take bow and arrow and come out on the hunt. It is the wild-goose moon. Maybe we bring home a fat wild-goose, if the Manitou smile."

"I know one thing," said Stephen. "I could never hit a wild-goose, even if I saw one."

"Come and try," said Kewakcum.

The food used so wastefully while abundance prevailed was now nearly exhausted, and every one was on short rations again. Waneton and the other hunters has gone off to search for bears or moose. Any small game, therefore, that the boys might chance to bring in would be most welcome.

Kewakcum had with him an old dog, left behind by the hunters, named Wees, or "the fat one." Nunganey was also going on the hunt. Nunganey had a sly, crafty face, not open and kindly, like Kewakcum's, and Stephen had felt vaguely that he did not like him, without any special reason for his aversion. Now he wished that Nunganey were not going with them. But, as that he could not help, he took his bow, threw his quiver *(to which Kewakcum had added three more arrows during Stephen's illness)* over his shoulder, and started off into the woods with the other boys. In dress and appearance he was as much an Indian as they, save for his curling yellow hair and pale skin, which yet showed even through the accumulated smoke and dirt of many days' residence in Indian wigwams.

Stephen noticed, as often before, how perfectly at home the Indian boys were in the woods. As they walked softly on, making no noise, their restless, glittering black eyes roved the forest over, and nothing escaped their observation. Especially did they note the least sign of life.

The boys came to a little brook; a brook that never saw the sun when the trees were in leaf, so dense were the woods through which it flowed. The ice still covering it was weakening and breaking in places where the current was swiftest.

Kewakcum pointed gleefully to some small tracks on a sandy stretch of beach bordering the brook, saying:

"Look. Brother Raccoon take little walk last night."

The boys followed the tiny tracks from the sand over the patches of snow and bare spots of earth, where often Stephen could see no track. But the Indian boys, trained from infancy to study the habits of wild animals, to note every faintest mark in woods or meadows, even to the brushing of the morning dew from the grass by a deer's passing foot, detected freshly disturbed dead leaves or other traces which showed them the trail. It brought them at last to the foot of an immense walnut, a giant of the primeval forest, straight and tall, its great trunk unbroken by a limb until the main branches sprang out, far above the ground.

Wees began barking furiously, for in the crotch above a fuzzy gray bundle was plainly to be seen, which Wees's sharp eyes told him were two raccoons, curled up closely together in this safe place, sleeping in the warm sunshine.

"Coons! Good," said Kewakcum.

"See Nunganey bring them tumbling down," said Nunganey, as he took careful aim.

The Indian boys and Stephen all sent arrow after arrow flying up towards this tempting prize, but their small bows were not strong enough to carry arrows so high, and back they bounded without reaching the game. Then the boys whooped and yelled, Stephen joining in the racket with 1 will, all rapping and pounding on the tree trunk. Wees did his best to help, by barking tremendously and leaping frantically up around the foot of the tree, as if with some wild idea of climbing it.

The boys hoped to scare the raccoons, and perhaps bring them down. But the raccoons lifted their heads and peered down at the enemy with cunning, crafty little faces. Then, seeing themselves perfectly safe, they curled themselves up in the same snug bundle, and calmly went to sleep again, unmindful of the tumult below.

"No good. Brother Raccoon too cunning," said Kewakcum, out of breath with his exertions.

"It's so aggravating to see them lying up there, just where we can't get them." said Stephen.

"Better go back to brook," said Nunganey. "Make trap for him. Catch Brother Raccoon tonight, when he goes down to drink."

The boys went back to an open spot in the brook, and set to work making a raccoon trap. They broke or hacked off several small saplings. These they laid one on another, near the spot where the raccoon tracks were thickest, driving in small posts each side to keep the saplings from rolling. The upper sapling they raised about a foot and a half, attaching a string to it, and setting it in such a manner that if the raccoon attempted to pass under, this upper log would fall on him and kill him. Brush was broken off and piled both sides, making an inviting pathway into the trap.

After much tugging and toiling, at last the trap was done.

"Wurregen," said Nunganey.

"Maybe fat coon walk in here tonight," said Kewakcum. "Coon meat heap good."

Next the boys searched under the walnut trees for any nuts that the sharp-eyed squirrels might perhaps have overlooked. Taking pieces of strong bark for shovels, they dug and scraped away the remains of drifts in shady nooks, for in such spots were nuts most likely to be found. The dozen nuts they found were smashed with stones, and the meats eagerly eaten, for breakfast had been scanty, and tramping about the woods had sharpened appetites already good.

Stephen could not help thinking:

"How free these boys are! They don't have to study Latin grammar or the catechism, or go to school, or church, or do anything. They don't have to work much. They are never dressed up, and made to be careful of their clothes. They roam the woods all day long if they please, and go wherever they choose. If they only had plenty to eat, I guess more than one white boy wouldn't mind being an Indian. Anyway, I have to be one until rescue comes. So I may as well try to make the best of it, and learn all I can about Indian ways, because it will be easier for me."

The boys now followed the brook down through a deep ravine to a pond made by a beaver dam. The beavers had worked hard in the fall, gnawing down small trees and saplings, dragging them to the brook, piling them up, and mortising the logs together with mud well pounded down by their strong flat tails, thus constructing a firm dam, which had set the water back over a level spot among the surrounding rocks. Many saplings stood in the pond, their trunks gnawed clean of bark as high as the beavers could reach.

The snow still lingering near the edge of the pond in the rock's shade showed tracks of some large animal, and Nunganey said:

"Ho, ho! Mukquoshim the wolf been to visit his brother the beaver. Eat beaver up if he catch him out."

"Brother Beaver too smart. He stay home and hide," said Kewakcum.

The pond in this shaded spot was still covered with ice, which was, however, weakening in places. Not a sign of a beaver was to be seen. Apparently there was not one within miles.

"No beaver here," said Stephen. "No good to stop here."

"Ho, beaver crafty; most as crafty as his brother the raccoon. He lie still, make no noise, but he here, all the same," said Kewakcum.

Wees meantime was sniffing eagerly about, running hither and thither in great excitement, as if he scented game.

"Brother Beaver much bashful. Knock on his door and invite him to come out," said Nunganey.

He and Kewakcum took sharp-edged stones or bits of rock, and proceeded to break the hollow ice where it lay up above the water, making several holes, Stephen imitating them and doing the same, though without the faintest idea why they did it.

Then the boys stamped and pounded around the banks of the pond until the earth sounded hollow under their feet.

"Ho, ho, beavers' house here," said Nunganey.

The Indian boys then dug down into the beavers' subterranean lodging-place, cunningly fashioned in the bank They had a brief glimpse of some dark object moving be. low, but when Kewakcum lay down and ran his hand into the hole, the little house was empty.

"Beaver take to water! Watch for him with sharp eye!" cried Kewakcum.

The beaver had indeed gone down the long passage leading from his den to the water, and had taken refuge in the pond. The boys knew that he could not live long under water, and hoped to catch him when he came up to breathe at one of the holes they had made in the ice.

They all lay down on the ice, each guarding a hole, keeping close watch for any sign of the beaver. Wees, to whom Kewakcum had given the hard command to "keep still" on shore, stood on the bank, wagging his tail briskly, head and ears up, full of liveliest interest in these interesting proceedings.

Suddenly Stephen gave a start, his heart beating fast. A small, slimy, shiny object projected from the water, at his hole in the ice! It was the tip of the beaver's nose.

This was all new business to Stephen, but he was determined to do his part. So he thrust down his hand, seized the beaver by the fore leg, and tried to pull him out, when the beaver set his sharp teeth smartly into Stephen's hand.

Stephen dropped the beaver, crying out for pain, jumping up and holding his smarting hand, which showed plain marks of the beaver's teeth.

"Papoose! Squalling papoose!" cried Nunganey, furious. "Papoose better go home, let Heelahdee strap him in cradle, carry him on her back!"

Kewakcum, too, was disappointed and provoked to thus lose the beaver when actually in their grasp, but was less severe than Nunganey.

"Pale-faces know nothing. No hunters," he said. "Indian hunter he know well that the beaver he bite if they catch him by the fore leg. Must always catch him by the hind leg."

So Stephen learned how to catch, or rather how not to catch, a beaver through the ice.

The Indian boys lay down again, patiently watching the holes, while Stephen went up on the bank and sat down by Wees, holding his smarting hand, thinking that he had had enough beaver hunting for one day.

After a long time the beaver again timidly thrust out his nose, this time as it chanced at the hole where Nunganey watched. Instantly Nunganey ran his arm down into the hole, managed to seize the struggling beaver by the hind leg, hauled him out on the ice and killed him.

Then who so triumphant as Nunganey? He hung the beaver's dripping body over his shoulder, marching on ahead, saying proudly:

"Nunganey mighty hunter. Nunganey take beaver skin to Montreal. Get big money. Buy himself iron gun and powder of the Frenchmen. Go on warpath before many snows. Ho, pale-face, he cry, like papoose. Boo, hoo, hoo!" he cried, mocking Stephen.

Kewakcum felt slightly jealous of Nunganey's success. Must he, the older of the two, go home at night empty-handed while Nunganey brought in triumphantly a fat beaver? Intolerable! He said with scorn:

"Nunganey he talk much, like squaw. Boast a heap, for one little beaver. Must think he shot a moose! Cosannip best Indian. He know enough to hold his tongue. Nunganey's squaw talk scares away game."

Nunganey's pride was somewhat taken down by this just sarcasm, and he said no more. But he improved sly chances to make up faces at Stephen, like a crying baby's, rubbing his hands in his eyes and sobbing a bit when Kewakcum was not looking.

"I hate him," thought Stephen, returning Nunganey's last grimace with flashing eyes of scorn. "Dirty red Indian, to think he is so much better than I. I know it is wicked to hate any one, but I do hate him, all the same. I can't help it."

The boys still followed the brook, which finally brought them out at a large pond, exposed to the sun, and partly free from ice. As they neared the pond, they heard from afar in the sky above a call,— "Konk, konk!"

The boys were filled with excitement, for all well knew that this was the call of a flock of wild-geese flying over to the north. What good fortune should they chance to alight at this pond!

The Indian boys hastily hid behind big trees growing close to the water, commanding Wees to lie down and keep still. Stephen knelt behind a small hemlock with low-growing branches, an admirable screen, through which he could still see the pond. All the boys placed their arrows in their bows, ready to fly. When the flock of wild-geese flew down into the silent forest to drink at an open place in the pond near the covert where the boys were hid, there was no sign of a human being anywhere about.

"Whiz" flew three arrows from the thicket. Up and away soared the frightened geese with wild cries, in swift line, up and on for the north. Out of the woods rushed the boys. Two wounded birds were seen floating on the water.

Wees now made himself useful, dashing down the bank out into the cold water, seizing first one bird, then the other, and swimming ashore with his prize in his mouth, shaking himself smartly after laying the game at the feet of his master with the satisfied air of one who says, "I did that myself,"

Nunganey hastened to lay hands on the larger bird, saying:

"Nunganey's swift arrow brought down this fat gander. He is Nunganey's."

"Why," exclaimed Stephen, almost too surprised to speak, "I shot him myself. I saw him tumble. That is my arrow sticking in his side. Is not that my arrow, Kewakcum?"

It may have been only a lucky chance, but at last Stephen had actually hit something.

"Ho, pale-face no hit moose, arm's length away. Gander is Nunganey's," said Nunganey, trying to draw out and hide the arrow.

Kewakcum was the larger of the two, and he had been disgusted by Nunganey's boasting. Moreover, Cosannip was his pupil, and he felt pleased at his prowess. He snatched the arrow from Nunganey, showed him Cosannip's private mark on it, and said:

"Nunganey's arrow far out there on the ice. Nunganey no hit even a goose's feather. Manitou angry because Nunganey boast, tell lies."

The other bird had Kewakcum's arrow imbedded in its bloodstained side. There was nothing for Nunganey to do but to make his way around on the ice and humbly pick up his fruitless arrow. Perhaps pride had turned his head and made him too confident, so that his aim had been careless.

He made no more faces at Stephen, as the boys now turned their steps towards home, and did not seem to have much to say. As for Stephen, in the joy and pride of having shot his first goose, and such a fine, big one, actually bigger than Kewakcum's, he found that he did not "hate" Nunganey so strongly as before, though still he did not like him. In the flush of success it is easy to forgive and forget.

"But he would have cheated me out of my gander if he could," was the thought still rankling in Stephen's mind.

Nor did his hand smart so badly. Joy and success are famous cure-alls. The gander flung over his shoulder hung heavily on Stephen's back as he grasped it by the feet, but little he cared.

"I wish my father and Sam could see this gander," thought he. "They would hardly believe that I really shot it myself."

When towards nightfall the boys appeared at the wigwams, each bearing such a fine trophy of their prowess as hunters, they were greatly praised. Their game was the more welcome as the men had not yet returned from the hunt.

The beaver was skinned and the skin carefully cleaned by Nunganey's mother and stretched to dry, for, as Nunganey had said, beaver skins brought a good price in Montreal. They were the Indian's ready money.

Heelahdee saved the geese feathers. The flesh was all boiled together, and when cooked divided equally among the women, children, and the one old man left in camp. A portion was saved for the hunters, which was fortunate, as late in the evening they came in empty-handed, having had no success.

Waneton was much pleased when he heard of this first success of his adopted son, Cosannip.

"Cosannip make mighty hunter before many moons have passed," was his prediction.

# 19

# LOST IN THE WOODS

THE boys were out early next morning to inspect their raccoon trap. It was aggravating indeed to find the saplings knocked out of place, the trap disturbed, but no raccoon to be seen.

"Brother Raccoon too sly; know too much; get out again," said Kewakcum.

He and the other boys rearranged the logs, making the trap stronger, Nunganey saying when they finished it:

"Brother Raccoon heap smart man if he get out of that trap."

Leaving the brook they struck off in a different direction from that traversed the previous day, towards some steep hills. Here they entered a wild ravine with abrupt rocky sides, great rocks and stones strewing the ground. The boys now walked cautiously, for this was a spot likely to be frequented by wild animals.

Presently Kewakcum and Nunganey both stopped, pointing with delight to a great tree whose trunk below the crotch was scratched and the bark worn and red.

"Brother Maqua, the bear, has slept in that tree. Maybe he there now," said Kewakcum, greatly excited. "Tell Waneton. He and the other hunters come and get him. Bear's meat good, bear's skin soft and thick."

The Indian boys walked on to investigate the woods further, their soft moccasins not even rustling the brown leaves on spots where the ground was bare. Stephen stood still a moment looking at the bear tree.

"I wonder how Kewakcum knew there was a bear in that tree?" he thought. "And, if there is one in there, how can the hunters get at him? I don't see."

At that instant Stephen heard just the faintest stir in the hemlock whose low growing branches swept down over the rock underneath which he stood. Once Stephen would not have heard this slight rustle. But already his ears were getting sharp to notice the least noise in the woods. Turning quickly and looking up into the hemlock's shade, he saw two bright eyes glaring at him through the green branches!

Stephen ran as for his life, and none too soon, for out from its covert sprang a large wild-cat with a flying leap, landing on the very spot where Stephen had been standing an instant before. Its gray fur was striped and mottled with black, and it resembled the domestic cat, only it was larger and heavier. Its tail was short and thick, and its legs and paws wonderfully big and strong.

Stephen heard the creature's fierce "meauow" as he dashed on, being joined in the race by Kewakcum and Nunganey, who heard the cat's cry, and, to Stephen's surprise, took to their heels so fast he could hardly keep up.

When the boys were well out in the open, and ventured to stop to catch breath, Stephen asked:

"Why did you run? I thought you would go back, and maybe we three could kill the wild-cat and get his skin."

"Ho, Cosannip he know not Brother Wild-cat, I guess," said Nunganey.

"Wild-cat hungry, very fierce, fight hard. Bows and arrows not strong enough. No kill him. He tear our flesh," said Kewakcum. "Better tell the hunters. They come for him and Brother Maqua tomorrow."

The boys rambled around in search of small game until the sun was high overhead, but not even a chipmunk did they bring down. They were ravenously hungry. At last they came to a small river which in this level spot where the current was sluggish had spread out into a pond. The surface, shaded with thick, overhanging evergreens, was covered with the winter's thick ice as yet unthawed.

"Ho, ho," cried Nunganey. "Try to break ice. Catch fish, maybe."

He and Kewakcum, aided by Stephen, pounded vigorously at the ice with sharp-edged stones, and finally succeeded in breaking a small hole through. Nunganey had brought fishing-tackle in his pouch, a line made of deer's sinew, with a sharp prong of iron attached for hook. This he baited with a tiny bit of dried meat he had saved for the purpose, and then dropped his line down through the hole into the dark, crystal-roofed cave where floated the fish.

Kewakcum and Stephen, having no fishing-tackle, set to work building a fire on shore under the lee of a high rock which made a good back to their fireplace.

"Do you suppose Nunganey will catch any fish?" asked Stephen.

"Maybe," answered Kewakcum. "Fish hungry after long winter. Dried meat taste good to them."

"Well, I know one thing; some fish would taste good to me, no matter who caught them," said Stephen, so hungry that he did not grudge even Nunganey possible success.

Kewakcum's prophecy proved correct, for not only were there fish in the pond, but they were hungry, and Nunganey drew out three of them before his bait was gone.

Stephen felt almost friendly towards Nunganey as he saw the fine fish tucked into the hot ashes under the fire just as they came from the pond, and especially when soon a tempting odor of frying fish filled the air.

The moment the fish might be supposed to be done, the boys drew them out from the ashes, stripped off the skin, scales and all, and dinner was ready. Once Stephen could not have been induced to eat fish cooked in this way unsalted. But now he ate his fish gladly, and when he had finished his last scrap, thought:

"How delicious that tasted! How I wish Nunganey had caught more."

The Indian boys wiped their hands on their hair, which was thickly greased as protection against rain, since they usually went bareheaded.

Stephen, not liking the fishy odor, went down to the hole in the pond, and contrived to wash his hands as best he could with cold water and no soap, drying them afterwards by rubbing them on his deerskin coat.

Nunganey viewed this action with high disapproval. He said:

"Cosannip is Englishman still. He no Indian. Pale-face never make good Indian."

"Wait," said Kewakcum. "Cosannip be good Indian before many snows. Cosannip shot fat gander. Nunganey shot none."

"Ho," said Nunganey, contemptuously. "That was nothing. Nunganey big fisherman. Catch fish for everybody."

The boys in their rambles had wandered so far from home that they now thought it wise to turn their steps towards the camp. After they had walked a while, Nunganey was struck with a happy idea.

"All take different paths home," he said. "Maybe scare up more game. Each find some. Maybe find more bear trees."

Kewakcum thought this a good plan. But Stephen remonstrated: "Cosannip does not know the way, cannot find it alone. I shall be lost in the woods, maybe, and some wild beast may eat me up."

"Ho, Cosannip he think he is a sweet morsel," said Nunganey.

"Cosannip must learn to find his way alone," said Kewakcum, who felt the responsibility of Stephen's training in woodcraft resting upon him. "The wigwams are there," he added, pointing east. "If Cosannip walk towards the sunrise, he have no trouble; come straight to wigwams."

Thus saying, the two Indian boys struck off into the woods by different routes, Kewakcum going to the north and Nunganey towards the south, leaving Stephen alone, to find his way home if he could.

He felt troubled and anxious as he hurried on, making his way between and around trees, bushes, and rocks, trying always to travel in the direction which Kewakcum had indicated. He kept his back to the sun, this being his chief guide. He tried to walk straight from it towards the east.

Another thing he had been taught by Kewakcum to observe: that the branches of the trees were thicker and more regular on the south side of the trunks, and that the north side was apt to be moss grown.

With these aids, for some time he felt pretty confident that he was keeping the right direction. But the sun began to sink low in the west, and still he seemed to be far from the camp. What should he do if night overtook him here in the woods haunted by hungry beasts? The thought made him try to hurry on faster, although rapid progress was impossible in the trackless forest.

The sun sank and Stephen's heart sank with it. Darkness slowly settled down over the lonely solitude. How vast, how solemn, how dreary seemed the silent forest! On every side its depths looked full of dark mystery.

"What shall I do? What can I do?" cried Stephen's heart in despair, as he stood still. It was worse than useless to keep walking, with nothing to guide his footsteps. Every step might be taking him away from the right track instead of nearer home.

Standing thus in despair, he heard in the distance a weird cry screeching through the dark, that almost curdled his blood. Some fierce wild beast, perhaps a panther, was abroad.

He knew that he was standing under a young tree, whose limbs grew low enough for him to reach, he thought, by great effort. Stephen had been noted among the Deerfield boys as a skillful climber. He lost no time now in using his skill. Feeling around and leaping up, by good luck he caught hold of a limb. He swung himself up, and tightly grasping the trunk, climbed with a speed born of fear high up among the branches.

He dared not shout or cry for help, well knowing that to do so would anger the Indians.

"Perhaps," he thought, "it will do no good, for the boys must be home ere this, and there can be no one else near. But I may as well try to make some one hear. It can do no harm, if it does no good."

He tried to hoot like an owl, having practised an imitation of that bird's note, winning Kewakcum's approbation, he saying with much satisfaction:

"Good. Cosannip fool the old Mother Owl herself by another winter."

"Whoo! Whoo!" rang out Stephen's child voice through the woods, in rather quavering tones. "Whoo! Whoo!"

He stopped to listen. Hark! Surely he heard an answering call. Yes, from far away came the hoot of a real owl, apparently.

"It's only an owl I've started up," said Stephen, "but I will hoot again."

Again he called, and again came the reply, this time sounding much nearer. Then Stephen heard something coming, something heavy it seemed, as it crashed along with clumsy step. What if it were a bear?

"Bears can climb trees," thought Stephen, his heart thumping in his ears. "O God, help and save me now!"

The stars shining brightly high overhead gave a dim light, now that Stephen's eyes were accustomed to the darkness. Straining his eyes in the dimness, Stephen was able faintly to discern a dark, large something approaching his tree. He clutched the limb tighter with convulsive terror.

Oh, what joy, what glad relief, when from below in soft accents came up Waneton's voice:

"Cosannip come down. Cosannip lost, no hollo. Good. Cosannip make good Indian; make mighty brave."

With thankful heart Stephen slid down the tree and followed silently on after Waneton, who bore on his back some huge object that made his step less light than usual.

As they came into the outer edge of the camp-fire's brightness, which lighted the forest depths far around, the shrill voices of Kewakcum and Nunganey rang out joyously:

"Ohoo! Ohoo!"

The boys were watching for Waneton, and gave the call always used to notify the camp of a hunter's return with game.

Waneton strode up to the camp-fire and threw down a fine deer, which burden he had easily borne on his back. The other hunters had already come in without game, so that Waneton's success brought great joy to the half-starved Indians.

Stephen followed Waneton quietly in, saying nothing to the other boys about having been lost. What was the use? He would get no sympathy. They would only despise him for his lack of woodcraft, and think it his fault rather than theirs. So thankful was he to be safely back that he cared not to talk about it.

Heelahdee and the other squaws made short work of flaying the deer, and soon had portions roasting on sharp sticks stuck around the fire and less choice bits stewing in the kettle hung over the blaze. The skin was carefully saved to be dressed and cured next day.

Heelahdee, in whose mind Indian superstitions still lingered, stronger when she was in the wild far from the influence and teaching of her priestly fathers, did not omit to present a thank offering of the warm meat to the Manitou who had given Waneton his good fortune. But, to make all right and sure, she also offered a prayer of gratitude to the Frenchman's God, using the little rosary given her by the good priest. This rosary, which always hung about her neck, was a much prized treasure.

While Heelahdee was busy at work and the men were eating, her youngest child, a strong baby nine months old, swaddled in deerskin and strapped in his birch-bark cradle, had been left standing leaning against a tree trunk near the fire. Feeling neglected, he now reminded every one of his existence by setting up a loud wail.

Waneton frowned, and Heelahdee flew to her papoose, laid the palm of her hand over his mouth, seized his little nose firmly between her thumb and forefinger, and thus effectually stopped the cry, holding the papoose's breath until he was half suffocated, when he was released. A little later the discontented baby ventured to cry again, his noise being again quickly stifled in the same way. But now his mother, while the men were eating, had time to nurse the baby. Satisfied and at peace he fell soundly asleep, and was hung up in his bark cradle from the wigwam pole for the night.

Stephen was sitting on a log near the fire, by Katequa, Heelahdee's daughter, about five years old, who was nursing a doll. This doll child, dear to the little mother's heart, was made of a small round stick over which a covering of thin deerskin was tightly sewed. A face was rudely painted on the upper end, and it was clad in Indian garments made of deerskin on which Katequa had sewed some pretty beads. A tuft of silky brown hair adorned the top of the doll's head.

"Pale-face woman's hair," Katequa had explained to Stephen, proud of this ornament to her doll.

Both children were equally hungry, and waited in enforced patience for the hunters to finish eating, when their turn would come to fill themselves with the roast and stewed venison which smelled so savory.

Not far away Kewakcum and Nunganey were passing the tedious time of waiting in a wrestling match, tumbling each other over and rolling around like two young bears.

Stephen, who had more than once seen Heelahdee stop her baby's crying as described, asked Katequa:

"Why does your mother do that? Why does she care if the papoose does cry a little?"

"Papoose must learn not to cry. Enemy hear, maybe, when Indians on march," said Katequa.

The power to slip noiselessly through the woods, perhaps through an enemy's country, or to steal on his camp unawares, was so imperatively necessary in the Indians' precarious life that even babies must be trained from earliest infancy not to cry. An infant's cry might imperil the success of a carefully planned raid, and cost many lives. So infants were taught to keep still from earliest years.

Waneton, who had sat eating by the fire, his ankles crossed under him, finished at last. Heelahdee then filled his pipe *(whose long wooden stem was handsomely carved and trimmed with feathers)* with what the Indians called "k'nick k'neck," dried leaves of the willow and other trees. With this she mixed a very little of the tobacco brought from Deerfield. This supply was almost exhausted, and Waneton would enjoy no more until he could trade some of his skins for tobacco in Canada.

As soon as Stephen had eaten he went into his wigwam and lying down was asleep almost before he could say his prayers. He was fast acquiring the Indian habit of both going to bed and rising with the birds.

It was important for the Indians to be out early in the morning, for then game was most plentiful and more easily tracked while the dew was fresh. Also in war, to be stirring early was a great advantage. Usually, unless there was a feast or council, darkness shrouded every wigwam soon after sun-down, save a tiny gleam, perhaps, from under the ashes covering the camp-fire. So it was tonight. Darkness and entire silence reigned.

# 20

# NUNGANEY'S TRICK

KEWAKCUM did not forget to tell his father of the bear tree which the boys had discovered in the ravine, and Waneton planned to start forth early next morning in search of the much desired bear. But a heavy rain storm set in during the night, and food being so plentiful Waneton decided to let the bear wait until a more favorable day before disturbing him.

In the gray dawn Stephen woke to hear the northeast wind howling dismally through the pines and shaking the wigwam. Sheets of rain drove against its sides and spattered down the smoke hole, and the smoke, beaten back by wind and rain, filled the wigwam, blue and dense.

The outlook for the day seemed dreary to Stephen. But at least there was one comfort, as he was reminded by the delightful odor of the venison which Heelahdee already had stewing over the fire; there was food enough, and good food, too. It was the Indian custom to eat but twice a day, at morning and at night. If, however, some guest chanced to arrive, food must always be offered, at any hour, and never be declined by the stranger. To decline to eat was to give great offense.

After the morning meal, Heelahdee, who was always hard at work, lost no time in dressing the deerskin, from which she meant to make a new shirt or coat for Waneton. She had already prepared a strong lye by pouring hot water into a bucket full of wood ashes. Into this lye she now dipped the skin, to aid in removing the hair. She then stretched the skin across a square, upright frame made of branches tied together at the corners and fastened to poles stuck in the ground. Before this frame she squatted, armed with an instrument made of a muskrat bone, whose lower edge was cut into sharp teeth, the upper end attached to a wooden handle. With this instrument she proceeded to scrape the hair from the skin.

When the skin was scraped clean she would rub the surface over with some of the deer's brains, and then smoke the skin in a smudge made of rotten wood. Deerskin prepared in this manner by the squaws remained supple. Even a thorough wetting did not harden or stiffen garments made from skins thus dressed.

Little Katequa was not yet old enough to work, happily for her, for Indian girls were obliged while still mere children to share all the squaws' hard toil. She had her doll, and was trying to build a minia- ture wigwam for it under the sloping edge of the big wigwam where it would not be crushed by the trampling feet of men, boys, and dogs, all liable to crowd in around the fire this stormy day.

"Cosannip will help Katequa," said Stephen.

Katequa had a plump face, soft skin, and bright eyes, and those cunning ways of a little child which often reminded Stephen of his brother Warham. It is natural to love some one, and Stephen, in his desolate surroundings, found comfort in talking and playing with this bright little one.

At Stephen's offer Katequa showed her white teeth in a pleased smile. She was fond of Stephen because he was always kind to her.

Stephen ran out in the rain to the wood-pile near by and brought in large pieces of bark.

"See, Katequa," he said, "these nice big pieces will make a better wigwam than those bits you have. You can't do anything with those."

Katequa looked on, happy, while Stephen stuck into the earth small sticks for poles, tying them together at the top in approved Indian style. These he covered with bark, leaving a pointed opening in front for the door.

"Cosannip, wait," cried Katequa.

She ran over to the corner where she slept, and from under the bed of boughs drew out some bits of deerskin, scraps her mother had cut off in making garments and given the little girl. The largest piece Katequa gave Stephen for a tent flap over the door. From the others she planned to fashion a new dress for her doll, to be embroidered with beads pulled from an old moccasin which her mother had also given her.

Stephen was quite happy while building this miniature wigwam, because he was busy, and, above all, because he was making some one else happy.

"It's all done now. Give your doll to me, Katequa, and let me put her inside," said Stephen, lying on the ground and pushing the doll into her new abode.

"See," said Stephen, "she sits up like a queen in there."

At this moment a moccasined foot was thrust close past Stephen's head, rudely kicking down the pretty wigwam. Stephen jumped up to see Nunganey, who had come softly up, unheard.

Katequa snatched her precious doll from the ruins and ran crying to her mother, who made a dash for Nunganey's hair, to punish him. But Nunganey's hair was cut (*as was Stephen's now, like that of the other Indian boys*) short on one side and left long on the other and, luckily for him, the short side being towards Heelahdee she could get no hold on the active Nunganey, who ducked and dodged with the supple slipperiness of the otter.

"Evil one!" she cried after him.

When at a safe distance, Nunganey shouted back:

"Cosannip turn squaw if he play with girls. Come out, Cosannip! Kewakcum says come."

Stephen did not altogether like to go out in the storm. But he felt it wise to obey Kewakcum, who was rather disposed, as an older boy and an Indian, to order around the captive white boy.

Once out, however, Stephen soon found pleasure in the warm spring rain, which was rapidly melting the last of the snow and thawing the ice still lingering on streams and ponds. It pattered on his bare head and trickled down his face, but Stephen did not care. The air was fragrant with a delightful spring odor, the scent of the bare earth, so welcome after the long, cold winter. In damp hollows the brown grass was fast turning green, and beside the brooks the willows were hanging out their pussies.

The Indian boys were not bothered with umbrellas or overshoes, or fears of getting wet or taking cold. If they were wet they simply dried their deerskin garments by the fire when they returned. Hardened by their manner of life, not made delicate by over-civilization or over-tenderness, they were able to enjoy a freedom that white boys might well envy.

The boys had set a trap for foxes over near the ravine where they had discovered the bear tree. Noticing tracks and suspicious marks around a hole which ran under some rocks, Kewakcum had said:

"Wonkussis the fox lives in there. Fox very sly, but Kewakcum slyer. Make a trap and catch him when he comes out of his house."

The three boys had built a trap of saplings before the hole, similar to their raccoon trap, only they had bent down a sapling and so fastened it with a long string to a bait of meat that should the fox venture to nibble the tempting bait, up would snap the sapling, taking, as the boys hoped, the fox with it.

They now went first to investigate this trap. As they came in sight of the rocks Kewakcum gave a whoop of joy, echoed by the others, for there, dangling high from the sapling's top, hung the body of a fine fox. The soft ground below showed many large footprints.

"See," said Nunganey, "the wolves try hard to get our fox, eat him up. But he hangs too high."

This plan of arranging a sapling to snap up, over traps for rabbits, foxes, and other small game, was always practiced by the boys, because thus their game was held high beyond the reach of the forest's hungry prowlers.

After taking down the fox, and resetting the trap in case he might perchance have a mate in his den, Kewakcum said:

"Now go look at raccoon trap."

The boys found the brook badly swollen by the spring rain and melting snow. Down every sloping bank and hillside poured streams of muddy water to swell its torrent. The pond was full of floating ice cakes, and had risen to the top of its banks, nearly to the point of overflowing.

"Maybe beavers drowned out. Catch some," said Nunganey.

"There, I thought I saw one's head sticking up over there," said Stephen, standing on the very edge of the bank, and pointing eagerly across.

"Cosannip go catch him," said Nunganey, giving Stephen a malicious shove.

Stephen lost his foothold on the slippery bank and fell headlong into the deep, icy water. He could not swim, for so great had been the danger of Indians around Deerfield, that it was not considered safe for the boys to venture over to the river, their only place for swimming. His last thought as the dark water closed over his head was:

"This is the end. O mother!"

He came up, gasping, to have a fleeting glimpse of Nunganey shaking with laughter on the shore, and of Kewakcum running down the bank dragging something. Then he went helplessly under again.

Kewakcum, with an Indian malediction at the mocking Nunganey, had brought a small log. Placing this down on a mass of ice cakes jammed closely together near the brink of the dam, he crawled cautiously out on the log and lay down.

The swift current, as Kewakcum saw, was bearing Stephen down stream. When next he rose, he came up near the jam of ice. Kewakcum seized him, managing to grasp his arm, and then dragged the half-drowned boy ashore.

The moment Nunganey saw that Kewakcum was likely soon to be at leisure to give his case the attention it deserved, he took to his heels and fled, followed by calls from Kewakcum of:

"Ho, ho! Nunganey better run! Kewakcum give him big whipping when he catch him."

Nunganey had also improved the opportunity to bag and carry off the fox, which was really the property of all three boys.

"Kewakcum he settle that business with Nunganey before another sleep," said Kewakcum, with an expression that boded no good for Nunganey.

Stephen, meantime, lay dripping on the shore, only partly conscious, unable to stir. Kewakcum rubbed him so that he could walk. While he was thus working over the half-drowned boy, help arrived. Above the pattering of the rain footsteps were heard, and Heelahdee came stepping swiftly through the forest to the rescue.

On his arrival in camp, Nunganey could not resist boasting:

"Ho, ho, Nunganey he no fear the English. Before many moons he go out on the warpath, and capture them easy, as Nunganey took this fox in his trap. Nunganey he sent the pale-face Cosannip down to live with the muskrats."

Katequa, chancing to overhear this boast, had run to tell her mother, who, forcing Nunganey to tell her the locality, had lost no time in hurrying to the rescue. She exclaimed as she saw Stephen's sad condition:

"Ho, the wicked Nunganey! He kill Cosannip. Waneton be very angry."

She lifted Stephen on her back, throwing her blanket around him and binding it across her breast as when she carried papooses in it, and stepped easily off, apparently not feeling her burden. Kewakcum sped ahead, anxious to catch Nunganey and give him what he deserved.

As Heelahdee bore her burden into her wigwam, Stephen heard faint mocking cries from afar in a voice he knew too well, apparently coming from a treetop.

"Papoose! Papoose! Pale-face papoose! Ya-ah-ah!" in imitation of a baby's cries.

Kewakcum started hotly off in the direction of the voice, but the crafty Nunganey was expert in hiding and was nowhere to be found. But Kewakcum unearthed the fox, hidden in the wigwam of Mahtocheega, the father of Nunganey, explained the case to Eeniskin, Nunganey's mother, a meek, patient squaw, who could do little with her son, and brought the game home, the flesh to be equally divided. The question of the ownership of the skin would have to be settled later.

Stephen was so chilled that his teeth chattered irrepressibly, and it seemed to him that he should never again be warm. But Heelahdee laid him by the fire, rubbed him hard, and made him a hot drink from the bark of a tree and certain roots well known to the Indians, given her by Notoway, the old medicine man. These she steeped together, Notoway meantime making mystic signs over the kettle, muttering charms and fingering the medicine bags adorning his necklace. After Stephen had drunk this compound she covered him with a soft bearskin, and at last Stephen, warm and comfortable, slept heavily.

In the evening he was aroused by, first, a tremendous barking from old Wees, and then loud outcries directly outside the wigwam, accompanied by a thumping and dragging sound. Was it possible? Yes, these outcries were in the voice of that great future warrior, Nunganey. Then was heard the voice of Kewakcum, in scornful accents, and somewhat out of breath, saying:

"Nunganey boasts; but he is only a squaw, a papoose one moon old. He no brave. He cries out when the battle goes against him."

Nunganey, driven by hunger, had ventured to slip back in the darkness, approaching the camp from behind, crawling on all fours out of the woods, hoping thus to reach his father's wigwam undetected. But faithful Wees had given the alarm, and Kewakcum, who was on the alert, had pounced upon him, and given him a sound drubbing.

Nunganey well knew he would get no sympathy at home. Indian boys were left largely to their own devices, to manage their own affairs and settle their own disputes. So long as they did nothing unbecoming a warrior, there was no interference. The drubbing Mahtocheega would consider only the fortune of war. But alas, Nunganey had disgraced himself! He had cried out like a pale-face, a squaw!

He hung his head, and hid among the trees until he thought his father was asleep. Then he crawled softly into the wigwam, groped about until he found the pot with some meat in it carefully left there by Eeniskin,——mothers cannot help a soft place in their hearts for even an unworthy son,——and then went to bed, his heart full of anger against Kewakcum and Stephen.

# 21

# THE BEAR HUNT

IT was several days before Stephen fully recovered from the shock and exposure he had undergone. Early the next morning after his misadventure Waneton and Mahtocheega set off for the bear tree, guided by the proud Kewakcum. Nunganey would not join the party, the relations between himself and Kewakcum being somewhat strained at present. He took his bow and arrow, and went off hunting by himself, saying to his mother:

"Nunganey go no more hunting with Kewakcum. Kewakcum he claim all Nunganey's game. Kewakcum no good. Nunganey great hunter. He go by himself, bring home heap of chipmunks, keep all their skins, make himself a coat."

And away he strutted into the woods, trying to conceal his discomfort under a brave carriage. Knowing Kewakcum to be away, he felt safe, as he passed by Waneton's wigwam, in making an impudent face at Stephen, who sat out on a log in the bright sunshine. But little did Stephen care, for he had heard Nunganey's outcry the night before. He only looked at Nunganey and laughed, and Nunganey, as he passed on, knew well why Stephen laughed.

Little Katequa had a happy morning, for Stephen amused himself and her, too, by making a fox and geese board, and teaching her to play the game. He found a large piece of bark which was smooth and white on the inner surface. He chopped the edges off with Heelahdee's hatchet to make it square. Then with a bit of sharp iron, one end of which he heated in the fire, he rudely traced the outlines on the board.

"Go, Katequa," he said, "to the brook and bring Cosannip a handful of pretty pebbles, the smallest you can find."

Katequa gladly ran down to the brook and soon came back with her little deerskin pouch full of pebbles, shaking it merrily to make them rattle as she ran. From these Stephen chose smooth white pebbles for the geese, and a larger black one with sharp corners, which he held up to Katequa, saying:

"See the hungry fox. Have a care, or he will eat up all Katequa's pretty white geese."

"No, no," cried Katequa, merrily; "Katequa's geese pick fox's eyes out with their sharp bills!"

She sat down beside Stephen on the log, her face very earnest, as she tried hard to play the game exactly as Stephen directed.

Waneton and Mahtocheega on reaching the ravine decided that the boys' suspicions were correct, that undoubtedly a bear had been enjoying his winter's nap in the hollow of the great elm. The important question was, had he already left the hollow, or was he still snugly snoozing within it?

Although it was yet rather early for bears to come out, still the spring sun shone with such inviting warmth it was not impossible that Brother Maqua might have been tempted to desert his winter quarters.

"Kewakcum climb up and see if bear in hole," commanded Waneton.

It was clearly impossible to climb the huge elm, which ran straight up, thirty feet without a limb to the main crotch. But Kewakcum's quick eyes saw, even before his father pointed to it, a slender young tree, with frequent branches, growing near the larger one. Up this he went, foot following hand from limb to limb, with the nimble activity of one who had climbed so many trees in pursuit of birds and nests that he was almost as much at home in a tree as a squirrel. He carried with him a long, sharp-pointed stick, which he placed up in the branches above him as he ascended, thus managing to take it to the top of the tree.

He climbed so far into the tree's slender top that it began to bend and sway perilously under his weight. Keeping on the side towards the bear tree, he let his weight bend the treetop towards the hollow where it was hoped the bear might lie concealed, until he could reach over into it with his long stick

Waneton and Mahtocheega stood below, looking anxiously up. They saw Kewakcum run the stick over into the elm's hollow, and thrust it down with sharp prods. A muffled growl was heard.

"Wurregen!" cried Mahtocheega; "Maqua still sleeps on his couch!"

"Kewakcum make bear come forth!" shouted Waneton.

Kewakcum again prodded hard down into the soft furry bundle in the hollow beneath. A growl was heard, then another, louder and fiercer.

"Maqua wake up, open his eyes," said Mahtocheega.

Kewakcum slid part way down the sapling, then, seizing the end of a pendent bough, swung out and dropped lightly down, landing on his feet.

"Kewakcum's name shall be changed to the Flying Squirrel," said Waneton, proud of his boy.

All now stood looking expectantly up to the hollow, where a snuffling and scratching was plainly to be heard. Presently a brown snout was thrust out, and finally the bear's head appeared, the sleepy eyes glaring around to see who had dared disturb his slumbers.

The hunters, guns in hand, were on the alert, ready to fire the instant the bear came out far enough to give them a chance. Kewakcum pleased himself by holding an arrow aimed on his small bow, pretending he was going to help slay the bear.

But the bear, after a moment's survey of the scene, decided that retreat was the wisest policy, and withdrew into his hole.

What was now to be done? Should the hunters try to compel the bear to come out of his hole, where they could get a shot at him, or should they cut down the tree?

Kewakcum, who felt much pleased with himself, because for the first time he had come forth to the hunt with the full-fledged warriors, and because his father had praised him, with sparkling eyes reaching towards his father's gun, cried:

"Waneton give Kewakcum his gun. Kewakcum he climb the tree again, shoot Maqua in his hole!"

Waneton looked with ill-concealed pride on his brave son, but Mahtocheega, with a frown, said gruffly:

"Kewakcum talk fool talk. How get bear after him shot? Better cut down tree first.,,

It was decided that the tedious task of cutting down the tree must be undertaken. Waneton swinging the Deerfield axe, and Mahtocheega armed with a sharp hatchet, went manfully to work, hacking away at the tree's huge trunk, cutting it on the side towards which they wished the tree to fall. As the cut became deeper, they were obliged to take turns, for only one could work.

It was a slow, tiresome task, as the elm was at least four feet in diameter, firm and solid at the base. The day was darkening towards night when at last the noble tree, which had towered proudly up for a century against wintry storm and blast, bowed its proud head, creaking and groaning as if a conscious creature, falling with a mighty crash that rent limbs from many a neighbor.

The two hunters had taken their stand near the spot where they judged the bear would come forth, while Kewakcum had prudently gone still farther away, on the opposite side of the tree from the hunters. But even experienced hunters cannot always foresee events, or make exact calculations.

The elm, instead of falling towards the hunters, veered and swayed off the other way. Its top branches switched against Kewakcum, knocking him down and half stunning him. As the trunk struck the earth with a resounding crash, echoing through all the silent forest, the bear, thrown out of his hollow by the shock, thoroughly awake now and mad with rage, bounded up and seized Kewakcum, who was struggling to his feet, holding him in a close hug.

Waneton and Mahtocheega could not shoot lest they wound Kewakcum. But prompt action of some sort was necessary. Seizing their long, sharp knives from the sheaths hanging at their belts, the two Indians flew at the bear, attacking him at close quarters, stabbing him again and again. The savage beast at this assault dropped Kewakcum *(who lost no time in rolling off till he could safely rise and run)*, and with angry growls tried to clutch and claw his new enemies.

It was a fierce battle for a few moments, until Waneton managed to seize his gun and send a shot, skillfully aimed, a little behind the bear's right shoulder, penetrating the heart. Poor Bruin, with an almost human groan, fell at last, yielding up his life to his enemy, man.

The Indians now stopped to regain breath and ascertain the extent of Kewakcum's injuries. One of his arms was badly torn by the bear's claws, and his sides ached from the tight clutch of the great paws. But he spoke up stoutly:

"Kewakcum can walk. He go home alone. Heelahdee cure him before many sleeps."

And away he went through the woods, walking rather feebly, but sustained by two thoughts: he was carrying himself like a brave; he had seen his father's look of pride and pleasure at his boy's manly bearing; and he would be the first to electrify the wigwams by the glad news of the bears capture. Moreover, he thought:

"Kewakcum show Nunganey where bear clawed him. Nunganey he never met bear in battle like Kewakcum."

Great was the excitement among the squaws and children when Kewakcum came in to the camp-fire in the dusk his bleeding arm swathed in his blanket, bringing the good news of a slain bear.

"My bold hunter," said Heelahdee, proudly and tenderly "come. Heelahdee will dress the wounds of her brave warrior, who met the bear and was not afraid."

"Kewakcum no cry out like Nunganey," said Kewakcum.

Heelahdee hastened to wash and dress Kewakcum's arm. The wounds were painful, and it hurt to have them touched, even gently. But Kewakcum took pride in bearing the pain without even wincing, looking at Stephen now and then as if to say:

"Observe the kind of warrior I am."

But little Katequa was crying enough for both.

"Why does Katequa weep?" asked Kewakcum.

"Because Katequa afraid. Great bear bite and scratch Kewakcum, almost eat him up."

"Stop peeping, foolish birdling," said Heelahdee. "Kewakcum is a brave. He cares not."

"Kewakcum kill bear if he comes around here. Katequa need have no fears," said Kewakcum.

The moment Kewakcum's wounds were dressed, Heelahdee and Eeniskin, accompanied by everyone able to bear a burden, even to Notoway, the old medicine man, and Nunganey, who had been reluctantly pressed into service, set out for the spot where the bear had been slain. They well knew that the carcass could not be left out over night for all the wild beasts of the forest to prey upon. The meat was too precious to be lost. As much as possible must be brought into camp that night.

Stephen and Kewakcum, being both on the invalid list, were left in charge of the fires and the younger children. Kewakcum ordered Stephen to bring a backload of wood to pile up near the fire, that the boys might easily replenish it from time to time. Then they sat by the high-mounting blaze, whose ruddy light brightened the thick pine boughs around, and shone far out into the dark recesses of the woods, and Kewakcum entertained Stephen by a vivid account of his adventure with the bear. It must be admitted the story lost nothing in telling. Had Nunganey been recounting the story, it is to be feared that Kewakcum would have accused him of boasting. But even an Indian boy does not every day have a personal encounter with a bear, and come out of it as valiantly as had Kewakcum.

When the squaws reached the spot where the dead bear lay, they found that the hunters had already flayed the carcass, and cut it up into chunks ready for carrying. The skin was rolled up and loaded upon one squaw's back, and everyone else took all the meat each could carry. The scattered fragments left behind would soon disappear before the wolves and foxes who were already lurking in the bushes around, ready to pounce upon the feast as soon as the coast was clear.

There was great cheer that night when this fine supply of meat was brought into camp. The squaws at once put great pieces roasting by the hot fire which the boys had kept blazing. Stephen ate of the roast bear flesh, a most appetizing food, till he could eat no longer. Then he lay down and went to sleep, even amid the noise of the feasting Indians, who celebrated their good luck by chanting loudly the Bear Song, to the accompaniment of the skin drum beaten by old Notoway.

By and by Stephen's heavy slumbers were broken. Someone was shaking him roughly by the shoulder.

"What is it?" cried Stephen, starting up. In his present precarious life, the slightest event might be a signal of life or death. "What is the matter? Has anything happened? Are we attacked?"

He saw Waneton standing over him, tall and grim, in the flickering firelight.

"Get up, Cosannip. Come and eat. Meat plenty now."

Stephen had not yet acquired the Indian habit of eating for the future, so to speak. When he had satisfied hunger, he stopped. He could not gorge now because by and by he should again be starving. So to Waneton's disgust he shook his head, saying:

"Cosannip had enough. Cannot eat any more now."

"Cosannip no Indian," said Waneton, turning on his heel, and going back to the scene of revelry, where hunters, squaws, children, and dogs were all happy in this rare abundance of choice food.

Kewakcum and Nunganey were holding their own nobly, like true Indians. No one could find fault with them. Kewakcum was not sparing the skeptical Nunganey full details of his adventure with the bear, winding up with the proud display of one of the bear's long, sharp, white claws.

Only a great warrior was allowed to wear a full necklace of bear's claws. But Kewakcum, in view of his manly conduct in the encounter that day, was to be allowed by Waneton to wear one claw on the necklace around his neck. This necklace was made of dried red berries strung on a slight deerskin thong, with here and there a dark polished fruit-stone interspersed. The white claw would hang in the middle, on Kewakcum's breast.

Nunganey's eyes narrowed with envy as Kewakcum proudly displayed the bear's claw, saying:

"When Indian look on Kewakcum he will see bears claw and know that Kewakcum he a brave."

This was unanswerable.

# 22

# CHANGED PLANS

SOON after the bear hunt Waneton and his band broke up camp.
The various small parties of Abenakis who had been scattered
about in the northern wilderness were to meet at an appointed place of
rendezvous, called by the Indians Cowas, meaning "a place of pines."
This was a large tract of pine woods near the mouth of Wells River in
what is now Newbury, Vt. Near by, stretching along the Connecticut,
was a tract of fertile meadowland covering many acres.

This was and had long been a favorite planting place for the Indians.
Here, as many a summer before, a large band had camped, to plant
the meadows with corn. It was also easy from this spot for the warriors
to vary the monotony of life, while the squaws were cultivating the
corn crop, by forays down the Connecticut. The Connecticut made a
convenient highway for their canoes right into the heart of Deerfield,
Hadley, Hatfield, Northampton and Springfield, that cluster of thriv-
ing settlements growing up along the river below.

Already since the bloody assault upon Deerfield in February, another
successful raid had been made on these settlements, and the settlers
were again reminded of the need of renewed caution when the young
leaves put forth on the trees.

On May 11th Deerfield was again destined to feel the Indian
presence, though only one family suffered. John Allen and his wife,

who lived at the bars in the common fence surrounding the pleasant meadows south of the settlement *(at the place thence called to this day "the Bars")*, were surprised and slain by a squad of Indians. No doubt these Indians belonged to a band bound for Northampton, for the next day, May 12th, Pascommuck, an outlying hamlet of five families in Northampton, near the foot of Mt. Tom, was surprised by a band of Indians aided by a few Frenchmen. All the inhabitants, thirty-seven in number, were taken captive. The invaders packed up plunder, and with their captives hastened off towards the north.

No sooner did the news of the assault on Pascommuck reach Northampton than a company of horsemen, led by Captain John Taylor, started in hot pursuit, with the usual disastrous result. The Indians on finding themselves pursued knocked all their captives in the head, except five or six. Of these, three managed to escape. The others were taken by the Indians to Cowas.

The breaking up of Waneton's camp made the usual lively scene. Squaws were hard at work, children running about, dogs barking, a general scene of tumult and confusion, as skins were torn from wigwams and all possessions packed for travel. There were now great bundles of skins on hand, the product of the winter's hunt; skins of bear, beaver, otter, fox, and wolf, in which consisted the Indians' wealth. The deer and moose skins were largely kept for their own clothing, and used also for strings, for moccasins, for many personal wants, but other skins were usually taken for trade to Montreal.

As Heelahdee had a great store of skins, her packs were large. She herself not only carried an enormous bundle of skins, but also her papoose, who having outgrown his bark cradle, was now borne in a fold of the blanket on her back. A big bundle was packed on Stephen's back, held on by a carrying strap of deerskin whose broad part rested on his forehead. So big was the pack, that after it was bound on he could not arise without assistance.

But once up he staggered along, managing by great effort to keep up with the company as they trailed along through the woods towards the northeast. Even the warriors were obliged to bear packs, so great was the wealth of the band in skins. Up hill and down, wading through brooks and small rivers, climbing over fallen logs, pushing through dense thickets, on and ever on marched the Indians, with steady, tireless pace.

They travelled without halt all day until towards nightfall. They were now nearing the Connecticut River. Stephen felt unable to pull himself on any farther, and feared he should fall by the way.

"Ho, ho, Cosannip," said Kewakcum from behind, noticing Stephen's faltering step. "Keep up strong heart. Soon the Indians reach their old camping grounds at Cowas. Most there now."

"Cosannip very glad," answered poor little Stephen, bent over under his burden.

The night shadows began to darken down in the forest. Suddenly Waneton and Mahtocheega, who led the band, paused, seeming to listen intently. From afar was heard the howl of wolves, seeming to draw nearer and nearer to the ears strained in listening.

A moment more, and the Indians, to Stephen's surprise, burst out into answering howls. Soon down a hill in the shadowy forest three Indians were seen approaching, led by Teokunhko the swift.

"Ho, ho, Teokunhko," said Waneton. "What brings Teokunhko towards the sun-setting?"

Teokunhko and his friends gave Waneton news that plainly disturbed him and Mahtocheega not a little. They had come to meet and intercept this expected band, to tell them that all the Indians were deserting Cowas in alarm. An Indian family camped in that vicinity had recently been attacked and slain by an Englishman aided by friendly Connecticut Indians. How large the attacking force, or what its further designs were, the Abenakis did not know; but they were thrown into great alarm by this wholly unexpected attack. They had considered themselves entirely safe, feeling that the English would not dare molest them after the crushing blow dealt at Deerfield the previous winter. They were now breaking up camp at Cowas, and departing in all directions for safer quarters.

Such was the tidings brought by Teokunhko. Waneton and Mahtocheega conferred. Then Waneton ordered the squaws, "Make the camp here where Waneton stands."

The band had happened to halt in the edge of a wood, on the bank of a small brook, a favorable spot for camping. The squaws cut wigwam poles, and Stephen, tired as he was, had to drag a backload to the camping spot, and also help bring pine brush for the beds, and wood for the fire which Kewakcum and Nunganey were starting.

In a short time, the wigwams were up, the fires burning the skins stowed away under the edges of the wigwams, and the Indians as fully settled and at home as if they had been dwelling there all winter. The pots were hung over the fire and a little of the small quantity of bear's meat still remaining was cooked in honor of the guests, who were more than ready to bear their part at the feast, provision having been short at Cowas.

The next morning proved the truth of Teokunhko's report, for a large party of Indians came down from Cowas. As Stephen stood watching them, he recognized with a shudder several of the savages who had been active in the attack on Deerfield.

He noticed one in the rear who seemed to be approaching him; a tall, thin Indian, who walked feebly, as if perhaps ill. Stephen drew back in alarm, as he saw that the sunken eyes were fixed on him. What could this Indian want of him?

"Stop, Stephen. Don't you know me?" cried a feeble voice.

At sound of English speech, Stephen stopped his flight, and looked more closely. Through the dirt and smoke and smears of paint he now detected a white skin. The smile stretching back the thin lips seemed familiar. Could this be his old soldier friend Jacob Hix?

"O Jacob, can it be true? Is this really you?" cried Stephen, running to meet his old friend.

"I suppose so," answered Jacob, "though I feel so little like my old self that sometimes I doubt whether this poor carcass I still drag around be really mine or not. I'm glad that you are still alive, Stephen, and in fairly good condition. I've often thought of you, and wondered how you were faring."

"Where is Deacon Hoyt?" asked Stephen, looking eagerly about for his other Deerfield friend.

"Alas!" said Jacob, shaking his head mournfully, "the good deacon is gone. He died at Cowas for want of food,— starved to death, in plain English. Our masters have had little food themselves, and have given us none. For some time we have had absolutely nothing to eat but such roots as we could manage to find for ourselves. The deacon was too far gone and too heart-broken; he couldn't stand it. He said he was glad to go and be at rest. As for me, you see how it is with me."

Stephen looked with deepest pity on the ghastly pale face, sunken cheeks, and thin form of one whom he remembered so well as a ruddy, strong, jovial young man. Now he was reduced to skin and bone, a mere shadow of his former self.

"I will run and ask Heelahdee to give you some bear's meat," he said. "Sit down, Jacob, and wait till I come back."

He ran eagerly to Heelahdee with his story. But Heelahdee shook her head and looked sober.

"Bears meat almost gone," she said. "None left for Indians pretty soon unless Waneton and the hunters have luck in the hunt."

Stephen could get nothing for Jacob until night, when Heelahdee gave him a small piece of meat for his own supper. Stephen took this to Jacob, saying:

"You eat it, Jacob. I am not so very hungry, and maybe there will be some for me tomorrow morning."

"No, no, Stephen, I can't take the food out of your mouth," said poor Jacob, looking longingly at the tempting morsel. It was so long since he had tasted meat!

In the end Stephen insisted on dividing the meat with his starving friend. It was but little more than a good mouthful for each. But it relieved Jacob's faintness, and Stephen was happy because he had at least done his best to help Jacob.

During that day more English people came into camp, for the Indians fleeing from Cowas brought down with them Mrs. Jones and her niece Margaret Huggins, who had been captured at Pascommuck, and Mr. Bradley, Hannah Eastman, and Daniel Avery, who had been taken prisoners at Haverhill.

These unhappy captives could hardly credit the tale, when Jacob called their attention to what seemed a little Indian boy, looking just like the others running around the camp, dressed in fringed deerskin coat, leggings, and moccasins, his hair cut short one side, left long the other, darkened with charcoal, his sunburned face further discolored with smoke and dirt.

"Do you see that little boy yonder?" asked Jacob.

The captives regarded with faint interest the small Indian, until Jacob added:

"That is little Stephen Williams, son of our good Deerfield minister, Rev. John Williams."

"Can it be possible?" exclaimed Mrs. Jones. "We all shuddered over the cruel slaughter and destruction at Deerfield, and above all, at the carrying off into captivity of the godly Mr. Williams and his family. How little did we think that the same calamity would shortly befall us! We in Northampton felt safe, it not being a frontier settlement like Deerfield which has had so often to bear the brunt of Indian attack."

"Poor little fellow!" said Margaret, "he seems to be turned into a true Indian. What would his good father say if he could see him now?"

"No one knows the fate of Mr. Williams and his other children," said Jacob. "Probably ere this the minister has fallen by the way, like Deacon Hoyt, unable to bear up under the awful hardships that captives must endure, as we know to our sorrow. Stephen may be an orphan now. The chances are that he will never get away from the Indians."

"I try hard not to lose my faith in God under these awful trials," said Mrs. Jones. "But I cannot see how God can suffer such cruel happenings to befall His people. To say nothing of our own hard case, how can He suffer an innocent child, son of such godly parents and ancestors, to fall into the hands of these barbarians, to be reared a heathen! I cannot understand it."

Her motherly heart yearned over the boy, and she would gladly have helped him, had she not been so powerless. She often watched him playing with Kewakcum and Nunganey, going off hunting with them, bringing wood and lugging water from the brook for Heelah-dee,—in dress, habit, even speech, apparently as much an Indian as his comrades.

"It is wicked, a cruel shame," she often said to herself.

As for Stephen, he was cautious about being seen holding much conversation with the white captives, because he found that Wane ton and the other Indians were jealous of such intimacy. He was so helpless in the Indians' hands it seemed his wisest course to keep their good-will,—at all events, not to irritate them.

One day Mrs. Jones, Margaret, and Hannah Eastman were all at work under the direction of their squaw mistresses, trying to dress a deerskin. The skin was stretched tightly on a frame standing outdoors near the wigwams, and the white women were laboriously trying to remove the hair with the sharp bone instruments which the squaws had given them to use.

The June sun shone hotly down, and the women toiled hopelessly at their hateful task. Mrs. Jones was so heated, so weak with hunger

and tormented with thirst as she worked on, that at last she ventured
to ask her squaw mistress if she might go to the brook for a drink.

"Go," said the squaw. "Pale-face squaw no good, too weak. Cannot
work like the Indian squaw. Indian blood red, makes heart strong.
Pale-face blood white, weak, good for nothing."

Mrs. Jones cared little for these scornful remarks, so long as she was
free to go. She went down to the edge of the bright little brook, purl-
ing along its rocky channel in the sunlight as merrily as if there were
no such thing as trouble in the world, and stooping over, scooped up
handfuls of the pure, cool water to quench her burning thirst. Then
she laved her hot forehead and cheeks in the stream.

It was a rest to be even for a moment here in the woods alone,
away from the sight of her Indian mistress, and from all the hateful
sights and sounds of the camp. It seemed possible to believe again in
the existence of God, here in the peaceful silence. His voice seemed to
speak in the solemn murmur of the pines, to say to her heart:

"Wherefore, My child, dost thou doubt? Knowest thou not I am
ever with thee, closer to thee than thine own self; that nothing, not
even death itself, can take thee out of My hand?"

Comforted and reassured, a look of peace softened the woman's
worn, troubled face. At that moment she heard footsteps, and turning,
saw Stephen coming down to the brook, bending under the weight
of a large brass kettle, the very kettle brought from his father's house.
He must fill it with all the water he could possibly carry, and tug it
uphill to the camp-fire.

"Ah, my poor child, let me help you," said Mrs. Jones. "At least I
am stronger than you."

Stephen was truly grateful. Mrs. Jones filled the kettle, and then
taking hold one side the handle, helped him carry it up the hill. Her
English speech, her soft voice and loving tone, reminded him of his
own dear mother.

"Tell me one thing, ere we reach the camp, Stephen," said Mrs.
Jones, earnestly. "You look so much like a true Indian that my heart
misgives me. Can it be that you have already forgotten the Christian
teachings of your pious father and sainted mother? Alone so long with
the savages, have you become one in heart? Have you ceased to pray?"

Stephen looked earnestly at his friend, tears filling his eyes.

"No, Mrs. Jones," he said, "I pray every night before I go to sleep, and every morning when I first waken, as my father taught me. That is all the comfort and help I have now, you see, so I am not likely to forget."

"You give me great joy, Stephen, and take a load off my heart," said Mrs. Jones. "Cling steadfastly to that faith, Stephen, and I do not believe God will forget or forsake you. Dark as our future looks now, if we can still trust in God and lie, as it were, in the hollow of His hand, I believe help and deliverance will yet come, though we cannot see how it be possible."

They had reached the camp-fire, and no further talk was feasible. But Stephen's childish heart was helped and strengthened by these first words of Christian faith he had heard for many weary weeks, spoken as they were by one also in the same deep trouble. Yes, it must be true,—help would come, sometime, somehow. He would try to keep up heart.

He needed all his courage, because to his other troubles were often added petty persecutions by Nunganey, whenever opportunity gave that sly enemy a chance.

The three boys had worked hard, improving every opportunity, building a dam across the brook some distance above the camp. When the dam was done, it caused the water to set back into quite a deep pond, making exactly what the boys wanted, a fine swimming pool.

The great work being done at last, the boys went down to try the new pond, and Kewakcum bid Stephen undress, saying:

"Now Kewakcum teach Cosannip to swim, same as Indian boy."

The day was warm, and Stephen was glad, anticipating the chance to go into the cool water. As the Indian boys wore almost nothing, they were ready without delay, but it took Stephen a little longer to shed his garments.

Stephen's face, from constant exposure, going as he did without any head covering, was burned by wind and sun to a hue almost as red as the Indians'. But under his garments his skin was snow white still. Strange enough it looked, contrasted with the lithe, copper-hued bodies of Kewakcum and Nunganey. It looked odd even to Stephen himself, he was so used to seeing only red skins, and for the first time he felt almost ashamed of being white.

As for Nunganey, he affected to be overcome with mirth. He rolled on the grass with laughter, pointing at Stephen, crying:

"Ho, ho! See the White Frog! See the young Gosling! Nunganey make White Frog striped!"

So saying, he threw a handful of mud, plastering Stephen's back.

"Now White Frog handsome," cried Nunganey, laughing more than ever at his own smartness. "Nunganey paint the Gosling's feathers some more."

He stooped for another handful of mud. Kewakcum stood looking impartially on. Stephen must learn to fight his own battles. If Kewakcum saw him getting badly worsted, he would no doubt come to the rescue; but Stephen must learn to stand alone if he were ever to be a bold warrior.

Stephen's detestation of Nunganey sharpened his wits and gave him strength. As Nunganey stooped, Stephen gave a leap, sprang on him, and with a mighty shove sent him hurling headlong into the pond.

"Ho, ho," cried Kewakcum in delight. "The brave White Panther too smart for Nunganey!"

Nunganey came up, sputtering:

"Ho, White Frog no drown Nunganey. Nunganey no care. He fish. He live in the water. White Frog no swim. See Nunganey the fish swim."

And around and around the pond he paddled, ostentatiously displaying his skill. Kewakcum had also gone in, and was circling around, his shining red body as much at home in the water as an otter's.

"Come, Cosannip," he cried to Stephen, still on the bank. "Come in. Kewakcum teach Cosannip to swim quick, before night."

"Yes, go swim, Cosannip," cried Nunganey, who had slipped ashore, giving Stephen a sudden push, sending him in his turn headlong into the deep water. As Stephen could not yet swim, his case might have been serious had not Kewakcum come to his aid.

Nunganey meantime was dancing a sort of war dance of triumph on the bank to celebrate his victory over Stephen. But suddenly a howl of pain rose from him. In his delight he had stepped inadvertently into a yellow jackets' nest, and the enraged insects were darting furiously at him on all sides with their sharp stings.

Stephen would have been more than human boy could he have helped laughing at this sudden discomfiture of his enemy, and laugh he did, while as for Nunganey, he dived into the pond up to his neck to rid himself of his tormentors, and was less rampant after this, fearing that Kewakcum would call him, as he promised to do, "Man-stung-by-the-wasp."

The strongest desire of Stephen's heart, ever since he could remember,—that is, since he was six years old,—had been to learn to swim. Now he was also spurred on by his wish to put himself out of Nunganey's power. He bent all his energies to doing exactly as Kewakcum directed, and made such headway that Kewakcum was proud of his pupil, and when at last the boys reluctantly left the pond, said:

"Cosannip be better fish than Nunganey the howler before the Strawberry Moon gone, if he keep on."

As the summer days went on, between swimming daily and going, like the Indian boys, naked from the waist up in the hot sun, Stephen was fast losing the white skin which had seemed to the Indians, and almost to himself, a sign of weakness.

Waneton and his band lingered in this camp until the middle or last of July. Provisions continued scarce. Their chief food came from such roots as they dug up, and the inner bark of birch and other trees,—food with little nutritive qualities, but sufficing to keep them from utter starvation. Happy did Stephen and the others count the day when they chanced to find a few half-ripe strawberries.

At last came the time when Waneton and his comrades broke up camp, and "set away for Canada," With them went Stephen Williams, not knowing what fate awaited him. Often he thought, as he toiled wearily on through the wilderness to the north:

"Is my father alive? Shall I ever again see him and my brothers and sisters? Shall I ever escape from the Indians' clutches? Or must I live with them all the rest of my life, and become at last an Indian chief like my captors?"

Made in the USA
Middletown, DE
19 August 2022

70757910R00111